Return to the Isle of the Lost

ALSO BY MELISSA DE LA CRUZ

DESCENDANTS

The Isle of the Lost

THE BLUE BLOODS SERIES

Blue Bloods

Masquerade

Revelations

The Van Alen Legacy

Keys to the Repository

Misguided Angel

Bloody Valentine

Lost in Time

Gates of Paradise

The Ring and the Crown

#1 *NEW YORK TIMES* BEST-SELLING AUTHOR
MELISSA DE LA CRUZ

BASED ON *DESCENDANTS* WRITTEN BY
JOSANN MCGIBBON & SARA PARRIOTT

Disney • HYPERION
LOS ANGELES NEW YORK

For information address Disney•Hyperion,
125 West End Avenue, New York, New York 10023.

First Edition, May 2016
10 9 8 7 6 5 4 3 2 1
FAC-020093-16060

Printed in the United States of America

Library of Congress Cataloging-in-Publication Control Number: 2016932666

ISBN 978-1-4847-5071-1

Reinforced binding

Visit www.DisneyBooks.com
and www.DisneyDescendants.com

THIS LABEL APPLIES TO TEXT STOCK

For Mattie,

my hero

And the

C.H. Class of 2025,

Go Vikings!

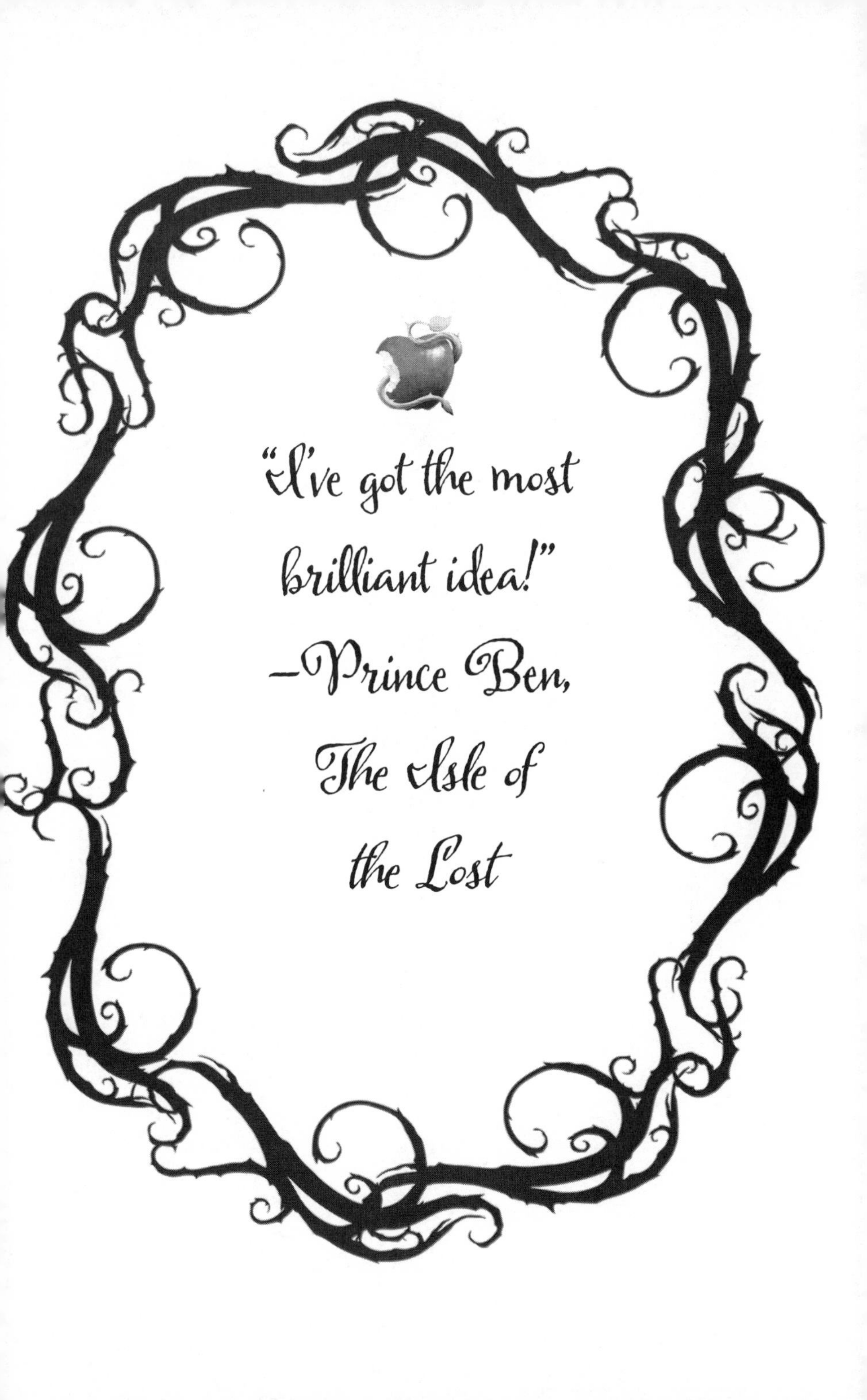

"I've got the most
brilliant idea!"
—Prince Ben,
The Isle of
the Lost

Disney's Descendants

Once upon a time, after all the happily-ever-afters, when all the fairy tales were supposed to have ended, came a new beginning when the teenage children of the most evil villains in the land were sent from the remote Isle of the Lost to the majestic kingdom of Auradon.

As you surely have heard, Mal, Evie, Jay, and Carlos, the descendants of Maleficent, Mistress of Darkness; Evil Queen, infamous for her sleep-inducing apples; Jafar, grand vizier of avarice; and Cruella de Vil, harridan extraordinaire, were sent far from home to learn how to be good.

After childhoods spent learning to be just the opposite, the villains, being villains, had other intentions.

Mal and her friends were tasked by their evil parents to fetch Fairy Godmother's wand and use its power to return the villains to their former glory and rain vengeance on their enemies.

However, after arriving in Auradon, these young villains were soon flummoxed by the friendliness of the natives and the abundance of sugary treats in this new land. They found themselves struggling between carrying out their sinister mission and enjoying their new, deliciously cookie-filled life.

Were they falling in love with Auradon while plotting its demise? Mal was certainly falling for someone—the handsome prince of her dreams, Prince Ben, whom she'd spelled into falling in love with her, only to realize she didn't need magic to capture his heart. Ben was as smitten as she was, and there was more to him than his brilliant smile, for he also had the heart of a king.

When the time came for Mal and her friends to make their move on Fairy Godmother's wand during Prince Ben's Coronation, it was not Mal who grabbed it and caused the chaos that followed, but Fairy Godmother's own daughter, Jane. As the invisible barrier over the Isle of the Lost shattered, magic returned to the villains in full force, allowing Maleficent to escape. The evil fairy turned into a fire-breathing dragon, terrorizing all of Auradon, determined to claim the wand as her own.

But Mal, Evie, Carlos, and Jay stood together, and it was Mal who won the battle and wielded the wand. In the end, her power for good was greater than her mother's talent for evil.

Mal and her friends are back at their studies at Auradon Prep . . . and Maleficent is now a tiny lizard, reduced to the size of her heart.

And this is where our story begins. . . .

The "Good" Life

"Like all
dreams, well,
I'm afraid this
can't last forever."
–Fairy Godmother,
Cinderella

chapter 1

Tale as Old as Time

If Mal had to pick what she liked most about Auradon, it would be hard to choose just one thing. She could probably spend a whole day cataloging everything that didn't stink about her new school. For one, it wasn't housed in a smelly, damp dungeon like Dragon Hall back in the Isle. For another, it was a surprise to find she actually enjoyed learning about a variety of subjects instead of just plotting evil schemes. She was particularly fond of her art classes, where she happily painted canvases full of mysterious foggy landscapes and gloomy dark castles instead of the peaceful sunsets and still lifes of fruit favored by the rest of the class. Why anyone would want to paint something as boring as a bowl of fruit, Mal would never understand.

She was sitting at a long table in the great room in Auradon Prep's library, a cheerful, bright space with high ceilings and banners with the school colors hanging from the ceiling. Mal was trying to do homework for a change, but was too distracted by the people-watching as students kept filing in and out between classes. Plus, her Goodness Appreciation essay was putting her to sleep. So she looked out the floor-to-ceiling library windows instead, at the manicured lawns where she played croquet (well, made fun of people playing croquet might be more accurate) and the patch of shady oak trees where she and her friends often ate lunch.

Yeah, life in Auradon was good; better than an unexpected makeover before midnight, or an endless feast presented by dancing plates and cutlery; better even, than being invited to a baby princess's christening.

"Happy?" a voice asked, snapping her out of her uncharacteristically dreamy reverie.

She blushed and smiled across the table at the handsome boy who smiled back at her from behind his swoop of golden-brown hair. "What makes you say that?" she asked.

"You look . . . positively delighted," Ben said, tapping his pencil on her nose to show he was teasing.

She raised an eyebrow. "I was just thinking what a

scream it would be to glue a fake nose on Pin," she said, meaning Pinocchio's son, who was a nervous first-year.

Ben chuckled, his eyes shining. He was a good sport.

Okay, so if Mal had to pick what she liked *most* about Auradon, she would probably have to admit it was the boy sitting across from her. Ben, son of Belle and Beast, was not only the kindest person she had ever met, but was easy on the eyes (um, make that *very* easy) and smart too. More importantly, while Mal was the polar opposite of Auradon's many perfect princesses, he liked her anyway. This made her feel as warm and cozy as her favorite beat-up patchwork leather jacket, which was much more her speed than ruffles and sequins. While she'd rocked a ball gown for his Coronation, she was glad she didn't have to wear one all the time. Talk about itchy.

Ben smiled and went back to doing his homework, and Mal tried to do the same, except she kept getting interrupted by friends who came by to say hello when they saw her in the library.

"Hey, Mal! Love your outfit today!" said Lonnie with a big smile. Ever since she'd learned the truth of the villain kids' deprived childhoods on the Isle of the Lost, Mulan's daughter was especially sweet.

"Mal!" cried Jane. "Will you stop by later and help me with my Fair Is Fair homework? I can't get the equation right." Jane was often nervous about doing things correctly, especially after the disaster she'd caused at Ben's Coronation. It was a lot to live up to having Fairy Godmother as your mother, especially when she was also the headmistress of your school.

"Thanks, and sure!" said Mal. "Anytime!"

"Look who's so popular," teased Ben, when the girls were out of earshot.

Mal gave a dismissive wave. "Everyone's just glad my mom didn't turn them all into dragon toast." She nodded toward the guarded, double-locked doors at the end of the room that led to Maleficent's new prison. "Not that I blame them." Joking helped assuage some lingering guilt about her mother's behavior; not all transfer students had to deal with things like having their parents try to destroy everyone at their new school.

Where was the new student manual for that?

"All thanks to you," Ben said with a serious look on his face. "We didn't stand a chance otherwise."

"Don't worry, I'll figure out how you can all pay me back later," Mal said airily. She couldn't help but smile. "Although another rousing vocal performance in front of the entire school where you happen to mention your ridiculous love for me might just do the trick."

Ben smiled broadly. "Done! There's a tourney game this weekend for Castlecoming. I'll practice my dance moves."

"I can't wait." Mal laughed, tucking a strand of her bright purple locks behind her ear.

"Sure you won't be too embarrassed to be my date at the dance after?" he asked, beginning to hum the catchy melody.

"Yeah, I'll probably have to hide my face behind one of Mulan's masks," she said, then the floor underneath their feet suddenly began to vibrate and the whole room began to shake. Mal grabbed her books before they fell to the floor, and Ben gripped the edge of the table, trying to keep it steady.

"Another earthquake," Mal said. "That's the third one this week!" Out of habit, she looked over her shoulder again at the door to Maleficent's prison. Until recently, Mal had only felt the ground rumble like that when a great big dragon stomped around during the Coronation attack, so Mal couldn't help but associate earthquakes with her mother.

"Heard it's happening all over, not just Auradon City," said Ben with a frown. "But it's a natural phenomenon, don't worry. Tectonic plates rumbling underneath the ocean and all that."

"Well, I wish they'd stay still," said Mal. "They make me queasy."

"At least they go away quickly," said Ben.

Unlike some people, Mal thought, forcing herself not to look back at the prison door.

There were no aftershocks to this one thankfully, and an hour later Mal had already forgotten about it. Ben began to put his books away in his satchel and she glanced at the clock. It wasn't time for the dinner bell yet. "Leaving already?" she asked. "King duties?"

"Yeah, I have to cut the ribbon at the opening of the new Sidekick Recreation Center. Don't want them to feel overlooked." Ben shrugged into his blue blazer with the embroidered royal beast-head crest on its right-hand pocket.

"Don't you mean kick the ribbon?" Mal teased, but Ben didn't laugh back. She knew he took his royal responsibilities very seriously, and he meant to be a king for all of Auradon—sidekicks and villainy offspring included.

"Text you later?" Ben tugged at a lock of her hair.

"Not if I text you first," she promised.

Mal did a little more work, but stopped when she heard her phone buzz in her backpack. Thinking it was Ben, she picked it up, but it was a text from an unknown number instead. Strange. She clicked it open and read the message.

Go back where you belong.

Excuse me? she sent. *What's this all about?* She looked around suspiciously, but the library was full of Auradon students diligently working on their Virtues and Values term papers on computer terminals or else absorbed in their Kindness and Decency reading. This week's assignment was Snow White's *How to Keep a Happy Home for a Family of Seven (Dwarfs Optional).*

Mal looked back down at her phone, waiting to see what would happen next, a pit growing in her stomach. There was no reply for a long time, then the little wand at the bottom of her screen began to show sparks, which indicated that the recipient was typing a reply. Finally it appeared on her screen:

You must return to the Isle of the Lost at once! Before the new moon rises!

Who is this? she texted back, more irritated than scared.

You know who I am.

I'm M . . .

There was no more. Just "M." Who was M? Mal stared at the screen. Who demanded that she return to the Isle of the Lost? And why did she have to return before the new moon rose? And when would that be, anyway?

Mal could think of a few M's in her life, but there was only one M that mattered the most. The big one. Maleficent. Could her mother be communicating to her through text? She might be sitting in her lizard-size prison right now, but she was still the greatest evil fairy who had ever lived. Anything was possible, she supposed.

Of course Maleficent would want Mal to go home. Her mother had only planned to escape the Isle of the Lost because its invisible barrier kept her from her magic. She despised Auradon and its pretty forests and enchanted rivers. If Maleficent had succeeded in her vengeful plot, the entire kingdom would be as gloomy, dark, and wretched as the Forbidden Fortress by now. In other words, darker than anything her friends at Auradon Prep could imagine. . . .

That was not something she could ever let happen.

Mal read the mysterious text again, apprehension making her heart beat faster. She collected her things, determined to find her friends so they could help her figure out what was going on.

Mal had a feeling that her sweet life in Auradon was about to turn rotten.

chapter 2

Fighting Knights

Jay was used to dodging angry shopkeepers and furious bazaar merchants as they watched their precious wares disappear into the hands of the fast-moving thief in the red beanie and purple-and-yellow vest, so playing tourney was *much* easier than that. At least he didn't have to dodge rotten tomatoes and threats of dismemberment as he zigzagged his way to the goal, trying to keep away from the red-and-white-striped painted "kill zone" in the middle of the field. It was a perfect afternoon for practice, the sky a cloudless blue, the trees bordering the field lush and green. The stands were empty save for a few students hanging out with friends or doing homework, and the cheerleaders in their yellow T-shirts and blue skirts were having their own practice by the sidelines.

When the ground beneath him began to shake, Jay ignored it and ran left, caught the puck in his stick, and ducked past the loaded cannons, tumbling as he whipped the puck right into the net. He raised his arms in victory, skidding to a stop on his knees just as the rumbling vibrations ceased. A slow, satisfied smile grew on his face. His long dark hair was plastered to his forehead and neck, and sweat drenched his uniform. Earthquakes didn't scare him; nothing could stop him from running as fast as he could toward a goal.

All his life, he'd had to use his fleet feet and lightning-quick reflexes to nab items to fill the shelves of his father's junk shop, at the expense of others. But here at Auradon Prep, his talents got him a coveted varsity spot on the tourney team, and Jay was getting so used to riding his teammates' shoulders at the end of every victory that the novelty had almost worn off. Aladdin's son, Aziz, even teased that Jay should lay off the pumpkin juice a little or else he'd get too heavy to carry.

The cheerleaders practicing on the sidelines screamed Jay's name in appreciation. He jumped up and doffed his helmet to them, causing the girls to giggle and shake their pom-poms even faster.

Jay was walking over to the sidelines to grab his water from his gym bag when he noticed a crumpled piece of notebook paper among his things. What was this? He opened it up. In purple ink, someone had scrawled, *Run back to where you came from! Return to the Isle of the Lost by moon's end!*

What was that all about? And what about the moon? Huh?

"Hey, man, good play," said Chad Charming. The golden-haired, pampered son of Cinderella usually wasn't very nice to Jay, but maybe there was more to this handsome prince than a headful of carefully coiffed hair. Chad held out his hand. Jay took it, albeit suspiciously.

"Thanks, man," he said, stuffing the strange note in the back of his pocket.

"Then again, anyone can score off Herkie." Chad laughed, squeezing Jay's palm and nodding toward Hercules's son at the goal. "All brawn but flat feet, know what I'm saying?"

Herkie was as strong as his father and had the muscles to prove it, but he wasn't the fastest on the field. Even so, Chad was lucky he wasn't within earshot.

"You're saying you could have done it?" asked Jay, his hand still clasped in Chad's grip.

"Blindfolded," said Chad, still shaking Jay's hand forcefully up and down and smiling through his teeth. "See, the thing is, Jay, it's easy to dodge a cannon, but in tourney, you've got to watch out for what you never see coming." And with his trademark sneer, Chad twisted his wrist and flipped Jay over, sending him sprawling on the ground face-first. *Oof.*

"See what I mean?" Chad smiled. "Consider it a little coaching between friends."

"Oh, Chad, you're too hilarious for words!" Audrey, who had come up from the sidelines to coo at her boyfriend, tittered.

"*Hilarious* isn't the word I'd use," grumbled Jay, spitting out dirt. Did he say he was tired of being lifted on his team's shoulders? Well, he much preferred that to being thrown on the ground at the feet of an annoying prince.

"Are you okay, Jay?" Audrey asked, concerned.

"He's fine, babe," said Chad, slinging an arm over her shoulders, the smile on his face as cloying as the pastel sweaters he usually wore. "Come on, there's nothing to see here but garbage. Isn't that what you guys used to eat on that island? Our leftovers?"

Audrey gasped. "The poor things, did they really? That's disgusting."

"On Charming's honor," said Chad, leading her away. "Let's go, Princess, nothing to see here."

Chad used to be one of the best players on the team, but not since Jay arrived. The prince wasn't taking his displacement from the starting lineup very well.

Jay sighed, looking up at the blue sky. He had traded a life of skulking and thievery to play good guy at hero prep. Back on the Isle, Chad wouldn't be laughing quite so smugly if he knew how easily Jay could have swiped his watch, wallet, and keys during that handshake. But Jay was in Auradon now, and they frowned on those things, so he'd left them alone, even though the temptation had been great. It would only get him and his fellow villain kids in trouble, which is what Chad really wanted.

"Are you planning on lying there forever? The dinner bell's rung," said a voice. He looked up to see Jordan standing above him, holding out a hand.

"You came out of nowhere."

"Genie trick." She winked, looking down at him with a hint of a smile. She wore her dark hair up in a swoop, and her blue pantaloons were striking with her yellow leather jacket. She was soon joined by two other girls, the three of them looking concerned over his fall.

Jay took Jordan's hand and used it to help himself up. "Thanks."

"Don't worry about Chad, he's like that to everyone. Isn't that right, Allie?" Jordan said to the blond girl standing next to her.

The girl nodded. She wore a blue pinafore over a white blouse and had delicate features and a genteel manner. "He's almost worse than Tweedledum and Tweedledee."

"Definitely worse. My dad would have things to say about him, that's for sure," said Jordan, whose father, Genie, was a famously talkative fellow. "Are you sure you're all right, dude?"

"Nothing bruised but my pride," Jay told them, feeling better already.

"Then he did us a favor." The third girl laughed, fixing the tiny hat she wore sideways on her head. Freddie Facilier was one of the newer Isle kids, who had transferred over as part of the ongoing program to assimilate the villains' kids into the Auradon mainstream.

"Thanks a lot, Freddie," grumbled Jay.

"You're welcome," said Freddie.

"We're not all like Chad," said Jordan. "Some of us know that without you guys, all of Auradon would be Maleficent's minions right now."

"Goblins," said Jay. "Maleficent's minions are goblins."

"That would be awful," said Allie. "Green is quite a horrendous color on me."

The four of them walked companionably over to the dining hall, bumping into Ben, who was headed the other way. The girls swooned and curtsied at the sight of the young king.

"You missed practice," said Jay, bumping fists with his teammate. He and Ben worked well together, Jay usually setting up the shots that Ben would send flying into the goal.

"I know, I know, next time, I promise," said Ben, looking harried. "Coach is on my case."

"Our defense is really hurting. Offense too."

"Yeah." Ben sighed, craning his neck at the tourney fields longingly.

"Well, you better be back on deck when we play the Lost

Boys," Jay said. They were up against a strong Neverland team that weekend.

"I'll do my best."

Jay nodded. It occurred to him while talking to Ben that if his father, Jafar, was in Auradon, he would probably figure out a way to smooth-talk Ben into handing over not just the crown, but the entire kingdom. Whereas Jay only wanted to play tourney and hang out. Just went to show that sometimes the apple can fall far from the tree—or maybe in his case, that the baby cobra can slink away from the nest?

He wasn't sure, but he hoped it was true.

"Hey," Ben said, noticing Jay's face for the first time. "Hold on. What happened at practice? Did Chad do that?"

Jay shrugged. He touched the skin around his eye and felt that it was swollen. He wasn't a tattletale, but Chad must have flipped him harder than he thought. "Eh, it was an accident. I'm sure he didn't mean for my face to meet the ground *that* hard."

"I'll talk to him," said Ben, frowning.

"Nah, leave it. You've got bigger problems," said Jay. "I can deal with Chad." The last thing he needed was Chad telling everyone he had to go running to Prince Ben every time he ate a little dirt.

Ben looked as if he wanted to argue. He exhaled. "Fine."

"Headed to dinner?" asked Jay, motioning to the dining hall, where the tantalizing smell of Mrs. Potts's cooking filled the air.

"No, I've got king stuff."

"Your loss," Jay teased. "What's the use of being king if you can't even stop for a decent meal?"

Ben laughed. "Tell me about it. Catch you guys later. Take it easy."

"Bye, Ben!" the girls called.

"Ladies?" asked Jay, leading the group to the building and opening the door for them like the gentleman he was. For a moment, he remembered the anonymous note he'd found in his gym bag earlier and wondered what that was all about. Who wanted him to return to the Isle of the Lost?

But he didn't let it bother him too much as the girls fussed over his injuries. Allie promised to brew him a cup of her favorite tea as well as ask her mother for any of the Mad Hatter's crazy cures. Jordan cheered him up with fanciful stories of traveling via carpet, and how he should really try it for longer trips sometime, and Freddie suggested ways to get even with Chad. "I'd substitute whipped cream for a tube of his hair gel. That would show him, don't you think?"

Jay felt better already. Who cared about a cryptic note telling him he didn't belong in Auradon? And for that matter, who cared about caves full of molten gold and treasures as vast as the eye could see? As he entered the cafeteria in the company of his friends, Jay felt as rich as the Sultan of Agrabah.

chapter 3

Scorch in the Stone

It was true what Ben had said to Mal in the library. The kingdom's business waited for no man, not even the king. The United States of Auradon was a vast empire that held all the good kingdoms, from Triton's Bay in the west to Neverland in the east, all the way to the mountain lands up north and Belle's harbor village down south, and its governance was no small task.

After bidding goodbye to Jay and the girls outside the cafeteria, Ben opened his locker and exchanged his plain daytime crown for the more elaborate one he wore for official meetings of the king's council. Okay, so it probably wasn't the best idea to keep it in a school locker—being studded with irreplaceable jewels and all—but then again, this was Auradon, and nothing bad ever happened here.

No petty theft, no grand larceny, nothing. He once lost a penny and it was returned to him immediately with a second penny for interest.

That was how Auradon rolled.

Ben also made a note to have a word with Chad. Even if he knew Jay could handle it, his black eye bothered Ben more than he cared to admit. Ben didn't expect everyone to be perfectly good all the time, but he did expect the people of Auradon to *try* to do better. Otherwise what was the point of keeping the villains separated? They might as well all live under a dome.

It had been a few weeks since his parents had left for their retirement-dream-mega-kingdom cruise. King Beast and Queen Belle had gone off in the royal yacht, leaving him to deal with everything. He passed the tourney fields on the way back to his own palace, wishing that he'd had time for practice. But most of his free time went toward his packed royal schedule now—pinning awards on heroes at fancy receptions instead of hanging out with friends, welcoming dignitaries like the Fitzherberts, who were in town this week, rather than playing video games.

Sometimes, Ben felt older than his sixteen years. After presiding over the recreation center opening and shaking hands (or was it paws?) with many furry and funny little creatures—those sidekicks were actually pretty hilarious—he hoped he wasn't too late for the meeting. Just because he was king didn't mean he wanted to take advantage of people's time.

"Ready, Sire?" Lumiere asked, standing sentry in front of the king's conference room.

Ben nodded and smoothed down his lapels.

"The King of Auradon!" Lumiere announced as he opened the door with a flourish.

"The King of Auradon!" the assembled councillors replied. "Hail, King Ben!"

"At ease, at ease," said Ben, settling into his chair. The throne had been built to hold his father and it still didn't quite feel like his own. He looked around the long conference table, smiling and greeting his advisers. Lumiere had placed the usual plate of sugar cookies and a pitcher of spiced tea in the middle of the table, and he waited until everyone had taken a bite to eat and had something to drink before starting.

"Hello, Doc, is it just you today?" he asked, greeting his most senior adviser in the room.

The old dwarf nodded after taking a sip from his glass. "Grumpy sends his apologies, Sire, but he got up on the wrong side of bed and he's feeling out of sorts today."

Ben suppressed a smile and moved on to the next councillor. “And how are you today, Genie? I just saw Jordan on the way over.”

“Wonderful, couldn’t be better, Your Highness,” said the big, blue genie, giving Ben his trademark grin. “I’m glad the school allowed her to live in her lamp instead of the dorms. You know us genies, we need to be bottled up.”

Ben chuckled and surveyed the remaining seats at the table, and noticed several were empty. “Is this everyone for today?” he asked.

“Yes, Sire,” said Doc. “The Dalmatians are out touring one hundred and one colleges. Mary, Gus, and Jaq are busy since Cinderella is preparing for her annual ball, and so it’s just me, Genie, and the three good fairies today.” Flora, Fauna, and Merryweather, a trio of stout, middle-aged women in colorful pointed hats and matching dresses and capes, beamed and waved from the end of the table.

“Perfect,” Ben said.

“Shall we run through the issues and updates?” asked Doc, who peered up from his scroll, and blinked behind his spectacles.

“If you please.”

Ben leaned back in his chair, listening to the regular report on every aspect of his kingdom. After the horror of *The Incident with Maleficent*, it appeared life had returned to its regular serene rhythm. Although the kingdom’s scientists had noted a few unusual weather patterns of late—not just the rash of Auradon City earthquakes, but unexpected frost in the Summerlands and unusual lightning storms in East Riding, among other unseasonal phenomena. Ben noted their concern, but as he pointed out to the council, it wasn't as if anything could be done about the weather. He yawned, and as Doc droned on, he tried to keep his eyes open, and failed. He got a few winks when Doc loudly cleared his throat.

"Ahem," said Doc. "Excuse me, Sire." Having been trained by a life with Sleepy, he was well versed in all manner of waking up the suddenly asleep.

Ben sat up in his chair and blinked awake, embarrassed. "Sorry, what did I miss?"

"I was saying, that's all we have of the regular business. But now, if you please, we have ambassadors from Camelot here to see you. They said it was an emergency, so I slotted them in. I hope that's all right," said Doc. "They've come a long way."

Ben nodded. "Of course, of course. By all means, send them in."

Lumiere opened the door again and announced with great zeal, "The wizard Merlin, and Artie, son of Arthur."

Merlin, an old and wizened wizard in blue robes, and Artie, a young boy of about twelve, wearing a plain tunic that marked him as a squire, walked into the conference room.

Artie looked around, seemingly amazed by the sight

of Genie floating next to the fairies. Camelot had its own extraordinary inhabitants, of course, but Artie probably hadn't seen someone quite like him before. Genie noticed the boy staring in awe, and pulled one of his many ridiculous faces, sending Artie into a fit of giggles.

"Arthur sends his regards," said Merlin, bowing to the king and shooting Artie a quick glare. The boy bowed as well, but couldn't hide his smile. "He's busy dealing with the problem right now, so he was unable to join us."

"What seems to be the matter?" asked Ben.

"There's a monster in Camelot!" Artie interrupted.

Genie startled. "A monster?"

"Well, I think it's a monster," said Artie, abashed and defensive at the same time.

"What Artie is trying to say is that something is causing a lot of mayhem in town, scaring the villagers and setting fires," Merlin said. "It's become quite a disturbance."

"Is that so?" asked Ben.

"Yes. It's been a few weeks now, and we've tried to catch the creature, but it keeps evading our traps, as if it has disappeared into thin air. Days will pass, then out of nowhere, it attacks again. Villagers have lost sheep and chickens. Gardens have been trampled. Whole rows of cabbages at a time." Merlin took off his pointy hat and wiped his brow. "It's been a real headache. Arthur decided to stay in Camelot in case it returned while we came to seek assistance."

"How can we be of help?" Ben leaned forward, eager

to provide aid. This was so much more interesting than the news that villagers in the province his mother was from were complaining about the price of eggs once again. Singing about it too.

Merlin shuffled his feet. "That's why we're here, Your Highness. We've come to ask for permission to use magic to track down this creature."

"Ah, I see," said Ben. "Magic." He sat back in his throne.

"He means the real stuff too," Doc whispered in his ear. "Not just turning dresses a different color or giving someone a new haircut like my nephew Doug tells me is happening at school these days."

"Is there no other way to catch this monster?" Ben asked, frowning and tapping his pen on the table.

"We've tried everything and unfortunately, so far we haven't been successful," said Merlin. "We wouldn't be here otherwise."

"And you believe that with the use of magic you will be able to catch it?" asked Flora with a stern face.

"What if it doesn't work? What then? Magic can go very wrong, you know," added Fauna, adjusting her red hat as it slipped to the side on her curly gray hair. "As my sisters and I have seen firsthand."

"The consequences of using magic recklessly can certainly be very dangerous," agreed Merryweather, her face screwing up with concern.

The rest of the table murmured its agreement.

Merlin drew himself up to his full height. He wasn't much taller than a dwarf, but he was intimidating nonetheless. He shot the king's council a frosty glare. "Need I remind you I am the wizard Merlin? I am well aware of the dangers of magic, and it is my belief that I will be able to use it prudently to capture this infernal creature and send it away so it cannot bother us again. You have my word."

The council turned to its king.

"I understand, Wizard Merlin." Ben met Merlin's glare, and tried not to show how nervous he was. He was the leader here now; his father had left the kingdom's safekeeping in his hands. "I will consider your request, but will need to discuss it with my team before making a decision. Thank you for informing us about the situation in Camelot," he said carefully.

The old wizard nodded gruffly. "Come on, Artie, let's go find ourselves a chocolate chip cookie while we wait."

When they left the room, Ben turned to his councillors. "Can I do that? Let Merlin use magic in such a manner?"

"You can do anything you want now that you're king," Doc said. "You have absolute power."

And absolute power corrupts absolutely, Ben thought to himself. He needed to be cautious. "When was the last time magic of this level was used in Auradon?" he asked his advisers.

"Let's see, probably the last time was when Fairy Godmother created the dome that kept magic out of the Isle of the Lost. After that, it's been your father's and Fairy Godmother's policy that we learn to live without magic, even without a dome over our heads," said Genie. "It was hard to adjust to at first, but we managed."

"And we are better for it," said Flora with a sniff. "A little hard work never hurt anybody."

Ben agreed. Magic wasn't expressly forbidden in Auradon—but it was discouraged, and the kingdom was more orderly for it. It would be reckless to just disregard the policies King Beast and Fairy Godmother had put into place for the sake of one issue in a faraway kingdom. Even in the hands of careful users, there had been a few incidents when magic had gone awry lately. Genie was known to accidentally grant wishes to the wrong person when he left his lamp lying around. Even the three good fairies slipped every once in a while, often letting their generosity get the best of them. They had created a massive ice castle for Ben's birthday party one year, which was dazzling until it melted and caused a flood.

Merlin was one of the most powerful magicians in the land, and if he was allowed to use magic on such a large scale, who knew where it would lead?

Ben motioned to Lumiere to send Merlin and Artie back into the room.

"I have considered the urgency of your request," he told them.

"Thank you, Your Highness." Merlin looked hopeful and eager to get going.

Ben held up his hand. He wasn't finished. "But for now, I am going to reject your petition to use magic to capture this creature."

Merlin frowned and his face turned red behind his beard. This was certainly not the news he had been hoping for, and the old wizard was clearly used to getting his way. Artie looked particularly glum. The idea of defeating a horrible creature with ancient magic had obviously been an exciting one for the young squire.

Before Merlin could object, Ben continued. "I will travel to Camelot myself to assess the situation. I will leave with you first thing tomorrow morning." He would have to miss a day of classes, probably two, but hopefully he would be back in Auradon by the weekend. Besides, it sounded like an adventure, and before Mal and her friends had arrived, even Ben had very few of those in Auradon.

"Very good, Sire," said Merlin, elbowing Artie to bow like he did. "Let's just hope Camelot is still standing when we get there."

chapter 4

Never Read the Comments

As one who aspired to be the fairest of them all, Evie didn't need to advertise the fact by wearing the word *fairest* emblazoned all over her T-shirts, but it didn't hurt. She was seated at her desk in her and Mal's bedroom that afternoon, in front of their matching poster beds and frilly pink curtains that Mal so despised. The wood-paneled walls were decorated with the smiling portraits of Auradon's past princesses, as if to remind Evie of her goals. She brushed her long dark tresses until her blue highlights shone and pursed her lips, checking her reflection with her phone's camera. She tried out a few poses for

InstaRoyal, the latest lifestyle envy-inducer that was a big hit with the Auradon set. It was all about showing off the newest and hippest fashions in glass slippers (glass mules with puffy bows were all the rage) and the plush interiors of private carriages (plump satin cushions sewn by Cinderella's hardworking mice were the most popular upgrade). Even though she'd only signed up a few weeks ago, Evie already had a lot of "subjects" and enjoyed collecting their "bows."

Evie much preferred InstaRoyal to ZapChat, its grungier counterpart, which was all about sharing glimpses of Auradon's less-than-perfect side: photos of the tourney team chugging pumpkin juice, for instance, or embarrassing pictures of princesses kissing frogs—and not the type that turned into handsome princes like Prince Naveem either. She was scrolling through her royal feed when her phone began shaking in her hand as the floor rumbled with another earthquake, and she accidentally tapped on a photo. It was one that Doug had posted earlier from band practice that he'd captioned *Feeling Dopey!*

She texted him, *Hey, did you feel that? Shake, rattle, and roll. . . .* Unlike Mal, she'd gotten used to the occasional rumble.

Evie went back to her zapps and checked the comments on her photos to see if there were any new ones. In Auradon, the compliments were always plentiful and kind. Oooh, there was a new one on an old photo she'd posted of the four of them standing together and facing down

Maleficent during the attack at the Coronation. This was the moment when they had defeated the evil fairy with the power of good.

It had run in the *Auradon Times* and it was one of Evie's favorite pictures, so she'd re-posted it to her account. There was something so inspiring about seeing them bravely standing together while facing the great dragon face of Maleficent. It reminded Evie that even if they were from the Isle of the Lost, they were just as good and courageous as the princes and princesses they went to school with, and that during Auradon's darkest hour, it was the four villain kids who had been able to keep everyone safe.

She found the new comment and read it eagerly. To her surprise, it wasn't very nice at all and had been posted by a user she didn't follow.

There's no place for you in Auradon! Go back where you belong! Return to the Isle of the Lost at once! Before the young moon shows its face! it read.

Ouch. That was rude. And weird. What was the deal with the moon?

She was still staring at the screen when Doug appeared at her doorway. "What's up? Ready to grab a bite?" he asked, looking adorable in a bow tie and suspenders. He made the same funny face that he'd posted to his InstaRoyal feed.

Doug was no prince, but a prince for her own heart. He was the sweetest, nicest boyfriend a girl could ever ask for, and he could dance like nobody's business.

"Sure!" Evie said cheerfully, putting away her phone for now. She was still upset by the mean comment, but a girl had to eat. Evie knew she would feel much better on a full stomach and she could show the comment to Mal later. Mal would know what to do about it; she always did.

Speaking of Mal, she entered the room just as Evie and Doug were about to leave. "Evie! Glad I caught you. I need to show you something!"

"Oh, Mal, I have something to show you too, but we were just about to go grab dinner," Evie said apologetically.

"No, this can't wait," Mal said, shoving past Doug. "Eat later." Her green eyes were flashing dangerously and it was obvious that she was particularly annoyed. Evie hadn't seen Mal act this way since they'd first arrived in Auradon, when she'd scowled at everything. Even if she was in a rush, Mal shuddered at the sunlight streaming through the open window and closed the pink curtains once more, just like she had done on the first day.

Some things never changed.

Evie looked nervously at Doug, who had his eyebrows raised. "Go ahead, I'll catch up later," she told him. Somehow she'd already lost her appetite.

"Whatever it is, I can help. . . ." he offered, because that was the kind of guy he was.

Mal rolled her eyes and put her hands on her hips. "Sorry, Doug, but I have to talk to Evie privately. This isn't about *mining jewels*."

"As you wish. See you later, Evie," said Doug, who promptly left them alone, whistling as he went.

"So what's up?" asked Evie, turning to Mal and walking over to sit at her sewing machine. Doing something with her hands always calmed her down during stressful times.

Mal didn't answer immediately. She watched as Evie carefully pushed fabric under the needle. "Is that your Castlecoming dress?" she asked. "That color is pretty."

"Yes," said Evie. "You really think it's pretty?" she asked, momentarily distracted by the compliment and running a hand over the glossy fabric and smoothing out the stitches. The dress was royal blue, her favorite color, with a deep red bodice the color of poisoned apples.

"Very," Mal said.

"Yours is ready, I put it in your closet. Not as many ruffles this time, like you wanted. Okay, so what did you have to talk to me about?" Evie asked.

Mal removed her phone and swiped to the screen with the strange message. "This," she said. "Look."

Evie read the message, her face growing pale as snow for a moment. "Someone left the same message on my InstaRoyal account." She handed Mal her phone with the offending comment on the screen. Mal studied it, frowning.

"Who do you think it's from?" asked Evie, feeling goose bumps on her arms. That had to stop. Pebbly skin was so not attractive. "I checked and the user's anonymous, and their account is private."

"I have no idea," said Mal, biting her lip.

"And by the way, why does it talk about the moon?" asked Evie.

"I don't know. At first, I thought the comments were only meant to be mean. But since they mentioned the moon to both of us, I wonder if there is more to it than that. Maybe they actually do want us to return by a certain time?"

Evie read the message on Mal's phone again. "Yours says it's from M."

"Yeah, I see that," said Mal. "And my mother used to count moon days rather than day days. Evil-fairy habit."

Evie crossed her arms. In their world there was only one M that mattered. "It can't be from her. I mean, she's a *lizard*? Lizards can't type! How can she be M?"

"I don't know. Maybe it's not her," said Mal hopefully.

"But what if it is?" whispered Evie.

"And who else would want us to return to the Isle of the Lost so badly?" Mal said. "It has to be from . . ."

"Our parents?" Evie squeaked. "You really think so?"

"There's only one way to find out. You still have your Magic Mirror, don't you? Let's ask it to show us our parents. If my mother is able to get out of that pedestal and turn back into herself, maybe it'll catch her in the act."

Evie removed the shard of the Magic Mirror that her mother had gifted her with before she left for Auradon. "Show me Maleficent!" she demanded.

The gray clouds in the mirror's reflection parted to show

a lizard snoozing peacefully under glass. Both Mal and Evie exhaled, relieved.

"What about your mom?" Mal suggested. "Just to make sure?"

Evie nodded. "Show me the Evil Queen!"

But instead of showing Evil Queen happily tweezing her eyebrows or shading in the mole on her cheek, the mirror stayed cloudy. Evie tried again. "Magic Mirror in my hand, show me my mother, I command!"

Still, the mirror's cloudy swirls remained hazy and swirly. Evie shook it a few times, and even banged it against her lap for good measure. "This isn't good," she said. "It's busted. This has never happened before."

When she asked, the mirror wouldn't show them Cruella de Vil or Jafar either, remaining stubbornly gray and fogged in.

"How about asking it to show us Evil Queen's castle, Hell Hall, and the Junk Shop?" Mal suggested. "Maybe that will work."

Evie did so, and the mirror cooperated this time, but there was still no sign of any of the three villains. The castle was empty, Hell Hall abandoned, the Junk Shop deserted.

"That's strange," said Evie. "It's not like they go anywhere." She was starting to have a dreadful feeling about this.

Mal wasn't ready to give up quite yet. "Ask it again," she urged.

Evie tried, but no matter what, the mirror remained cloudy. "Maybe it's broken?" she asked hopefully.

"No, it was working otherwise," Mal pointed out. "Something else is going on, something that might be connected to the messages we received today."

Evie stared at Mal. "Are you thinking what I'm thinking?"

"That Cruella, Jafar, and Evil Queen are up to their old tricks on the Isle of the Lost and that Maleficent might be involved somehow? Totally," said Mal.

Evie found she couldn't breathe for a moment. She was glad she hadn't eaten anything, or else she would seriously throw up right now.

"We don't know who sent us those messages, but here's what we do know," said Mal, straightening her shoulders. She didn't look frightened anymore, and Evie took comfort in her friend's courage; it gave her back some of her own. "The villains won't rest until they exact vengeance on Auradon. . . ." said Mal.

"And it's possible they've hidden themselves until they can put their evil plan into action," Evie finished.

"Evie, we've got move fast," said Mal.

"On it."

"Let's go get Carlos and Jay."

chapter 5

Tangled Web

Back in Dragon Hall, it had been school policy that the library, otherwise known as the Athenaeum of Evil, was forbidden to the average student. Carlos de Vil had never been the average student, however. Most of the reading material he'd been able to find there had consisted of last year's TV guides for shows he'd never heard of and past issues of *Carriage & Driver* magazine. Knowledge was hoarded like stolen gold and plundered treasure, and was equally hard to come by.

But at Auradon Prep, the library and its abundant resources were free and open to all. After school, Carlos could usually be found in the library, admiring the leather-bound books on every subject, from *How to Keep Yourself Busy for Sixteen Years Alone* by Rapunzel to *Genie's Blue Planet Travel Guides: See the World in Three Wishes.* He would never get tired of the place.

But today he was holed up in the room he shared with Jay, seated on his comfortable bed with the blue plaid comforter around his shoulders as he stared at his laptop, ignoring the large-screen television and its many video games. The matching blue plaid curtains were drawn shut. As it turned out, like Mal, he preferred to work in a dark room. Carlos had been there all afternoon, so lost in his research that he'd missed tourney practice.

Carlos was a naturally curious boy, and when he wanted to understand how something worked, he didn't stop until he'd figured it out. For instance, when Auradon City was hit with several earthquakes in a row over the past weeks, he'd looked up the statistics and noticed that there had been more quakes in the last month than there had been in the last year. He kept meaning to bring it up with his Wonders of the Earth teacher but hadn't gotten the chance yet.

This time he wasn't merely curious, though. He was furious. Earlier that day, he had received a rather upsetting e-mail. Unlike most kids at Auradon Prep, Carlos wasn't very active on royal media—his GraceBook account only had one old post, he never sent ZapChats. He preferred the ease of his genie-mail account, which organized his e-mails like magic.

That morning, he logged in to see if the new video game he'd ordered (*Crown of Duty*) was on its way and discovered a new e-mail from an unknown sender. The message, like most anonymous messages, was mean-spirited, telling him to go back where he came from and return to the Isle of the Lost by moonset. While the e-mail itself had been annoying, it really irritated him no end that he hadn't cracked the e-mail sender's true identity yet.

Carlos figured he was smarter than the average troll, but the only progress he'd made was to unmask the server that had routed the e-mail, and so far he hadn't been able to hack through its security defenses.

"Dalmatians," Carlos muttered, frustrated enough to use his mother's favorite curse. "Sorry, Dude," he said, apologizing to the dog on his lap. Dude whimpered and Carlos scratched him behind his ears.

The rapid-fire sound of knocking on the door startled him. "Come in!" he yelled, and looked up to see Mal and Evie entering with dark looks on their faces.

He held up a hand as they crowded around his desk. He'd been expecting them for a while now. "Don't tell me. You've both received rude messages saying to return to the Isle of the Lost, haven't you? Which is why you're here? I got an e-mail today."

"How did you know . . . never mind," said Evie. Carlos was often a step ahead of them.

"Yes, we did," said Mal, pulling up a chair, giving Carlos

the details. "What've you found? Do you know where they're from?"

"Not yet," he said, his fingers flying over the keys. But he was getting close, he could feel it. He'd finally breached the first security firewall; now all he had to do was figure out the password. He tried to ignore the girls so he could concentrate.

"Isn't it weird that you got an e-mail, Evie got a comment on her InstaRoyal account, and I got a text?" Mal pointed out. "Whoever's behind it seems to know us pretty well."

Carlos nodded. "I'm barely on royal media, you only use your phone, and everyone knows Evie's always updating her feed. Do you think they reached Jay? He's never online and he's always losing his phone."

"I'm sure they found a way," said Mal.

"We think the messages might be from our parents," said Evie a little breathlessly.

That was not news he wanted to hear. "What! Why?" Carlos twisted around, suddenly seized with the fear that his mother, Cruella de Vil, with her wild hair and trademark screech, was right behind him.

Dude whimpered.

"Relax, they're not here, at least not yet," said Mal. Then she told him how Evie's Magic Mirror had been unable to show them the villains on the island.

"Well, call me paranoid, but lately I feel like she *is* near.

Like she's watching me somehow. I can't shake the feeling," he said, panicking as he imagined Cruella appearing at his doorway. While Maleficent might be able to turn into a dragon, Cruella *was* a dragon.

"Nah, you're just paranoid," said Mal.

Carlos chewed on this new information. "Maybe so, but you're saying there's really a chance they're behind these messages? Our parents? They want us to come back? But why?" he asked.

"Because they miss us and want to give us hugs?" said Evie. "I'm kidding, I'm sure my mom only wants to know if I'm keeping up with my weekly mud masks and facial massages."

"They want us to return so we can help them get their revenge on Auradon, of course," said Mal. "Defeat only makes villains try harder. I can just hear my mom now, saying *'You poor simple fools, thinking you could defeat me! Me! The mistress of all evil!'*" Then she cackled like Maleficent.

"You're scarily good at that," said Evie, shivering.

"Thank you, I think?" said Mal.

Carlos shuddered and turned back to his computer to try out a succession of common passwords. None of them worked. He stared at the blinking cursor. "Dalmatians," he cursed again. Then he realized if Mal was correct and the villains were behind the messages, there was only one way to find out for sure.

C-A-V-E-O-F-W-O-N-D-E-R-S, he tried. Nothing.

M-A-K-E-U-P was his next guess. He sighed with relief when it didn't work, and *E-V-I-L-L-I-V-E-S* turned up nothing either.

Gathering his courage, he decided to try one more password that would link the messages to their parents.

D-A-L-M-A-T-I-A-N-S, he typed.

The screen froze and for a moment Carlos was relieved that his hunch was incorrect, but after a second it came to life again, and green letters began scrolling across the screen. He'd hacked it. He was inside.

"Oh no," he said.

"What's wrong?" asked Evie, squinting at the screen. It was a Web site unlike any they'd seen before. It was more primitive and crudely designed, with no pretty icons or bright colors, only windows of black screens with green letters.

"The Dark Net," Carlos whispered, still staring at the screen, unwilling to believe it was true. "There's a rumor going around that after the dome broke when Maleficent escaped, the Isle of the Lost was able to start up a secret online network of their own. And I'm not talking about the kind of Internet where people share funny kitten videos."

"But we don't have access to the Internet on the Isle. We're cut off, remember?" said Mal.

"Maybe something happened when the dome broke open," said Evie.

"Anything's possible," said Carlos. "Especially during

that time when the dome let magic back onto the island." He looked up at them. "Supposedly since the Dark Net is effectively hidden from Auradon's servers, it's a way for the villains on the Isle of the Lost to communicate with each other. Think about it, on the Dark Net, they can hatch evil plots without anyone here knowing anything about it."

"So they use the Dark Net to send each other evil e-mails?" joked Mal.

"And post evil insta-messages." Evie giggled.

"I'm serious!" said Carlos. "It's not funny."

"You're right, you're right," said Mal, sobering. "With an online network, they can organize their evil schemes more effectively."

"Yeah, exactly, so I'm going to poke around, see what else I can find," said Carlos.

"But, Carlos, you just said the villains are behind it!" Evie cried. "Isn't that dangerous?"

"I would say Danger is my middle name," said Carlos cheerfully, warming up to the task as his dog slid from his lap to nestle at his feet contentedly. Now that he had a new thing to explore, he didn't feel as frightened. He could do this. "But my middle name is actually Oscar."

He saw their faces and muttered as he typed, "Hey, it could be worse, right? Mal, your middle name is Bertha."

"Unfortunately, yes. Anyway, see what you can find," Mal said with a crisp nod. "But I think we have to make plans to return no matter what."

"Return? To where?" Carlos asked, although he had a feeling he already knew the answer.

"To the Isle of the Lost, of course," Mal said as she rolled up her sleeves.

"But why? We might be falling right into a trap," Evie argued. "Isn't that just what they want us to do, whoever they are?"

"Well, we can't stay here—we need to find out what the villains are up to back home," Mal said. "Plus, I'm not going to be intimidated by whoever's sending these messages. We have to take the risk, or something like what happened at the Coronation could happen again."

"We sure do," said Jay, who'd appeared at the doorway, his face bruised and one eye swollen shut, holding up a crumpled piece of paper covered in purple ink. "Did you guys get one of these today about returning to the Isle of the Lost?"

"Old-fashioned note! Of course!" said Carlos, who couldn't help but be pleased at the cleverness of their mysterious nemesis.

"Sort of," said Mal as the other two nodded. Jay looked relieved.

"What happened to your eye? Are you all right?" asked Evie. "Do you need Mal to conjure an ice pack for that?"

"Tourney practice. It's nothing," Jay said, waving off their concern.

"But as I was saying, we have to go back home, because

we all know the villains won't rest until Auradon is reduced to rubble and we're all minions," Mal said fiercely, as if she would take on an army of them right now.

"Goblins," said Jay. "Maleficent had goblins for minions, why doesn't anyone remember that?"

chapter

Maleficent Dearest

After the group left Carlos to explore the Dark Net to see if he could find any more information on the villains' plans and whereabouts, Mal decided to visit her mother. It bothered her too much to think that the mysterious M in her note might actually be Maleficent and she wanted to see for herself that her mother was still a lizard. It was late when she arrived in the library, almost time for lights-out. The royal guards, trained in imperial battle tactics by Mulan, stood in front of the double-locked doors and barred her way.

"Really? You know it's me," Mal said. "Open up. Family

visitors are allowed under the royal decree," she reminded them like she did every time she grudgingly visited.

The guard on the left grinned. "Oh yes, I see the resemblance now, I think it's the forked tongue," he joked, like he always did.

"Ha-ha," said Mal, pushing her way inside.

The guard on the right grunted. "You have five minutes."

"I know," she said as they locked the door behind her and she made her way to the pedestal in the middle of the room with a glass dome sitting on top of it.

When she was a little girl, Mal had been very frightened of her mother. Maleficent was not the help-with-homework, bake-cookies type, after all. She was more the fearsome mistress who sent you on hopeless quests—like the one to retrieve her Dragon's Eye scepter—and she didn't take no for an answer.

Even so, these days Mal found it hard to believe she had once feared Maleficent. It was difficult to feel scared of something so small.

But the anonymous message from M had spooked her. Mal stared at her mother, who appeared to be sleeping. Under the glass dome, she looked like any ordinary lizard, harmless, cute even. But Mal knew better. No matter how harmless the reptile looked, it was still the Mistress of Darkness at heart.

So did Maleficent have some secret talent they didn't

know about? Would she able to transform back into herself after transforming to the itty-bitty size of her heart? Was the lizard in there *really* Maleficent? What if Maleficent was already gone?

Mal stared hard at the tiny purple creature that, when awake, had green eyes just like her mother to see if she could sense something different about it. But the snoozing reptile looked exactly the same as it did the last time she'd visited.

"Hey, Mom, can I talk to you for a second?" she said, careful not to tap on the glass. She'd heard lizards didn't like that.

The lizard was still, not even a flick of her tongue.

The handful of times when she'd visited Maleficent in the past, it was like this. She never got a reaction of any sort. Mal always found it hard to accept that this small, tiny creature held the soul of the most powerful villain in all the land.

"Did you send me this?" she asked, holding up her phone with the mysterious text. "Are you M?"

No response.

"It's only the two of us here, Mom, you can tell me if you've been changing back. In fact, it would be kind of nice to see you in your nonreptilian form," she said. Mal still wasn't above a white lie now and then.

There was no sign that the creature even understood a word she was saying.

Mal sighed. "I guess if you *were* planning something, you wouldn't share it with me anyway, right? Seeing as I'm the reason you're here in the first place." She rubbed her eyes. "But one day I'll find a way to get you out. You just have to promise me that you won't try to destroy everything again." Mal paused. "Okay, fine, you can cover Sleeping Beauty's castle in thorny vines. Have a little fun."

The lizard remained as still as the rock underneath it. The lights-out bell chimed and Mal reluctantly got ready to leave. "Fine, don't tell me anything. I knew this was stupid. You can't even talk."

Just then, the floor buckled underneath her from yet another earthquake. Mal swayed and struggled to keep her balance, her heart lurching in her chest. When it was over, she stared at the lizard suspiciously. "I don't know how you're doing it, but why do I have a feeling you're behind this too?"

Someone was skulking outside the door when Mal walked out, and she immediately tensed, prepared for an ambush. But there was no surprise attack, and the stranger had a familiar face.

"Hey, Freddie," she said, relieved to see her old friend from the Isle, and slightly embarrassed by her reaction.

"Hey, Mal, what's up?" said Freddie, graciously pretending not to notice how rattled she seemed.

"Nothing much," said Mal, then a thought occurred to her. "Hey, Freddie, did you get any weird messages or e-mails today?"

"Weird how?" asked Freddie.

"Anonymous weird?" said Mal. "Like maybe from someone from the Isle of the Lost?"

Freddie shook her head. "No. I don't think anyone even knows I'm at Auradon actually. Not our old gang back on the Isle, that's for sure. They probably all just think I'm cutting classes again."

"Right," said Mal. She'd only been in Auradon for a short time, but she'd almost forgotten how lax the rules had been back at Dragon Hall. But what Freddie said was interesting. Unlike the four of them, Freddie hadn't received a message to return to the island, which meant whoever had sent those notes only wanted the four original villain kids. But why?

"You got some kind of anonymous note?" asked Freddie.

Mal decided she could trust her. "Yeah, saying I should return to the Isle of the Lost, and Jay, Carlos, and Evie too. Isn't that weird?"

"Totally weird. What are you going to do about it?"

"I don't know yet," said Mal. "We're trying to decide."

"Well, maybe you should. . . . Go back to the island, I mean. See what's going on back there. I mean, it can't hurt, right?"

"You really think so?" asked Mal.

Freddie shrugged. "I know if I got one I'd want to see who sent it to me." Then she changed the subject and motioned to the heavily bolted doors and the armed guards standing sentry in front of them. "Is that where they keep your . . . ?"

"Yep, that's lizard rock," said Mal. "The one and only home of Maleficent these days."

"Phew, if that ever happened to my dad, you can be sure I wouldn't be sticking around just so he could yell at me when he turned back." Freddie shook her head, her pigtails bouncing. "And you shouldn't either. You know if she ever gets out of there, she'll come after you first."

Mal bit her lip. "You're not telling me anything I don't already know."

Freddie suddenly brightened. "But she'll probably never get out, so you'll be fine. By the way, if you do go back to the Isle, say hi to my dad for me." She clapped Mal on the back and went on her way, casting long shadows against the walls.

chapter

Friends of the Round Table

Camelot Heights was located in the northern part of the kingdom, and the city of Camelot was in its center, flanked by Sherwood Forest on one side and Eden on the other. Ben had made good on his promise and had been traveling all day with Merlin and Artie in the royal carriage, with a retinue of servants and footmen following behind in a regular coach. Ben decided not to use the usual king-size motorcade since Camelot's roads were too rough for cars, as most of its residents traveled by horse-drawn vehicles.

As soon as they set off, the old wizard was already snoring in the backseat, but Artie was awake and excited, trying out all the features of the carriage interior and playing with the sunroof, sliding it open and closed on a whim. "Dad won't let us update our carriage," he explained as he put on road-canceling headphones (carriage travel was notoriously loud due to wheel rumble) and eagerly flipped through every channel offered on the television screen installed above the back bench.

Ben settled in, amused, and let Artie have his fun.

The journey from Auradon City was a long one, taking them up to Summerlands and past Snow White's castle, where they would stop for the night before making their way into the Enchanted Wood, then across the river through acres of forest lands, and finally into Camelot. Ben tried to relax in his seat, and sent a few texts to Mal to let her know he was thinking of her. No luck, she wasn't responding, and so he closed his eyes and tried to rest.

A few hours after Ben, Merlin, and Artie left Snow White's palace the next morning, King Arthur's Castle crested high on the hill, proud and tall, its red towers glowing in the sun.

"Home," said Artie excitedly. "Looks like they knew we were coming." The turrets were flying both the Pendragon banner and Ben's beast-head sigil.

"I sent Archimedes ahead with the news so they could prepare," said Merlin, meaning his pet owl. He put his rumpled wizard's hat back on his head and scratched his beard. "What in Auradon is going on here?" he said as the castle gates opened for the royal entourage.

Ben yawned and took a look outside the window. The entire courtyard was filled with tents and crudely constructed shelters. "Is it always this crowded here?" he asked as they disembarked.

"No," said an irritated Merlin, stepping off the carriage and, in his haste, stumbling over his robes. "Something must have happened."

Artie jumped down, and Ben followed, eager to stretch his legs after the long ride. They were greeted by quite a sight—and odor. The scent of roasting meat and smoke filled the air as people huddled around unruly fire pits. The people of Camelot preferred to live as they always had, and eschewed many modern conveniences. All well and good, thought Ben, except a little deodorant never hurt anyone. It smelled like the Middle Ages in here.

"It looks like the villagers have moved from their homes to seek protection behind the castle walls," said Merlin, frowning. "The creature must have struck again," he muttered under his breath.

"Make way for the king, make way," Ben's royal guards ordered, clearing a path through the crowd to the entrance to the palace.

"King Ben!" the people cheered as men bowed their heads and women curtsied. "The King of Auradon has come!" he heard people whisper. "Hope has arrived at last!"

He waved back cheerfully, trying to ignore the nerves

fluttering underneath his confident smile. His subjects depended on him, and now he understood why his father had always projected strength and self-assurance. Apparently it wasn't as easy as he had made it seem.

"This way," said Merlin when they were inside the castle proper, where the great hall was also teeming with people lying in bedrolls and hay. The castle's lord chamberlain rushed to meet them. He bowed to Ben and whispered in Merlin's ear.

"They have prepared rooms for you in the east wing," Merlin said. "Arthur apologizes that he is not here to welcome you, but he is still out in the countryside, urging his people to head to the safety of Camelot, and expects to be delayed for quite some time. He hopes that in his place, you shall meet with his knights, who are aware of the latest developments in the situation."

"Thank you," said Ben. "Please tell Arthur no apologies are necessary and I look forward to speaking with his men."

"Sire, shall I go ahead and unpack and prepare your wardrobe?" asked Lumiere, who was traveling with Ben as his personal valet. The old Frenchman looked askance at the unwashed hordes and was probably wishing they were all back in Auradon's much more comfortable palace right now.

"Please do," said Ben as Merlin and Artie took their leave.

"Shall I set out the royal armor, Sire?" asked Lumiere,

meaning the old-fashioned metal one that was once his father's. "We brought it out of storage, it's polished and oiled."

"No need, I think," said Ben, inwardly grimacing at the thought of putting on the tin-can suit. "I might be in Camelot, but I am the king of this century, not the twelfth."

"Very good, Sire," said Lumiere with a smile as bright as candlesticks in the dark.

Ben chose to wear the same royal-blue suit he'd worn to his Coronation, with the gold epaulets and Auradon's crest on the sleeves. Lumiere had polished his traveling crown, so he looked and felt very much the King of Auradon as he was welcomed to the legendary Round Table, where Camelot's knights had gathered. The room itself was rather plain, with unadorned stone walls and dim lighting, but Ben couldn't help but feel excited when he pulled up a heavy wooden chair at one of the most famous tables in history.

The knights were a good-natured, chivalrous bunch, and Ben felt right at home in their company as they chatted about the latest pro-tourney scores. But the discussion took a serious turn when Merlin called the meeting to order and talk soon became heated as they argued about how best to deal with the creature plaguing their land.

"Yesterday the thing set fire to the forest, creating such a blaze that it almost reached Sherwood!" a young knight said indignantly. "We need to destroy it before it destroys anything else!"

"Too many people have lost their farms and houses to this thing," said another. "Good that Merlin is back, he can use his magic to capture it."

"Ahem," said Merlin, polishing his glasses with the edge of his long sleeve. "Unfortunately, we don't have permission from the king do to so. King Ben, I mean."

Ben looked around the table at their distressed faces and cleared his throat. "As you know, it is our belief that the use of magic at this level can be dangerous, and so I'm here to observe the situation before we decide to change the policies that have kept Auradon safe and peaceful so long."

"You know what's dangerous? The creature! That's dangerous!" cried a knight. "Sneaks around in the dark of night, taking livestock and setting fire to everything before disappearing in a cloud of smoke!"

"Merlin tells me that no one in Camelot has actually seen this creature?" Ben asked. "Is that still true?"

The knights shuffled in their seats and glanced at each other nervously. "Well . . . sort of," said the knight on Ben's left.

"It's dark. . . ." was one excuse. "It's fast. . . ." was another.

"But if we don't know what we're fighting, how can we prepare to fight against it?" Ben said. "We can't chase after shadows and smoke. We have to know exactly what it is that's attacking your lands. You have my deepest sympathies and every resource I can offer from Auradon, but before I can allow Merlin to use magic, I need to know exactly what we're up against."

Heads nodded around the table as the knights digested Ben's words. Merlin had Archimedes perched on his shoulder and the owl trained its bright eyes on Ben as it whispered in the wizard's ear. "The king makes a fair point," said Merlin, at last. "We must lay eyes on this creature before we can conceive of how to stop it."

Artie, who had been quietly listening in the corner until now, spoke up. "Dad said he saw a bunch of tracks in the forest by the river's edge near Eden," he said. "Maybe we should set up camp there tonight and see if we can spot it."

"Excellent idea," said Ben, who admired the boy's pluck. "We will camp tonight."

The royal entourage, along with Ben, Merlin, Artie, and a handful of knights, established temporary barracks in a clearing by the shore. Every night they waited for any sign of the creature, but two days passed and they didn't see smoke or fire, let alone any sort of mysterious beast emerging from the woods.

On the third evening, Ben scoured the river's shoreline, hoping that the creature would finally make an appearance. He was still unsure about allowing Merlin to use magic, and he knew the old wizard was growing impatient. King

Arthur was still abroad, warning his people to find shelter, although he couldn't be too pleased to have his castle overrun by his subjects.

But Camelot's monster wasn't Ben's only problem. It was Castlecoming on Saturday at Auradon Prep and he really wanted to play the tourney game and take Mal to the dance, and he was disappointed that it looked like he wouldn't make it back in time. But that was the boy in him speaking. The king's place was here in Camelot, at the edge of the forest, waiting for a creature to appear from the shadows.

In the wee hours of the morning, Ben was asleep in his tent when he heard a boy scream.

"It's here! It's here!" cried Artie. "It's a dragon!"

Ben dashed out of his tent and looked up at the sky, where, sure enough, a huge purple dragon was roaring, sending massive fireballs down to their camp and setting trees ablaze.

He felt his heart stop in his chest, for his worst fears had been realized. He had seen such a dragon only once before. . . .

chapter 8

X Marks the What?

On Thursday, a few days after he'd first discovered the Dark Net's existence, Carlos was running across campus as fast as he could, almost as if he were still scared of dogs and had a pack of them chasing him. His teammates on the tourney field watched him run and cheered him on. "Go, Carlos!" they yelled, thinking he was practicing for Saturday's game.

When he finally arrived at the girls' dormitory and made it up to Mal and Evie's room, he threw himself at their door only to find it open already. He tripped and fell, crashing hard on the floor, just barely able to save his laptop from hitting the ground.

"Carlos!" Evie said as she and Mal helped him up. "Are you okay?"

"Yeah, I'm okay," he said, getting to his feet. "I found something!"

"On the Dark Net?" asked Evie.

"Yes! Where else?" He sat on Mal's bed—which now had a purple coverlet over the white frills, and opened up his laptop to show them. "It's not good."

"Well, if it's on the Dark Net, we didn't think it would be," said Mal, reasonably enough.

Once again he brought up the black screen filled with green letters and began to move through the open windows, scrolling through the threads until he found what he was looking for. "Got it," he said. "Here!"

"What am I looking at exactly?" asked Evie, squinting.

"It's a forum. People go online and post things anonymously, mostly, um, complaining about things, being mean. You know what a troll is, right?"

"Yes, but I didn't think they could type," said Evie doubtfully.

"No, not a big goblin, like a person on the Internet who only says nasty things about people," Carlos explained.

"Nasty things?" Evie blanched. "Who would do that?" She had lived in Auradon too long now; she wasn't used to malice anymore.

"It's the Dark Net. The villain online underground, what do you think they'd post?" he pointed out.

"Puppies?" Mal said sarcastically.

Carlos looked ill. "I was digging around and I found this forum about something called the Anti-Heroes movement," he said.

Mal curled her lip. "Anti-Heroes? I don't like the sound of that."

"You shouldn't," said Carlos. "Because look at this." He typed in a few keystrokes and a colorful picture filled the screen.

"That's us!" cried Evie.

It was a photo of the four of them, and there was a huge red *X* on all of their faces along with the words *Join the Anti-Heroes Club Today!* scrawled in spiky red letters.

"Anti-Heroes. So they're anti-us? Are we the heroes?" asked Evie. "And the club is organized against us?"

"Looks like it," said Carlos grimly. "My guess is that the Anti-Heroes movement is a revolutionary group founded on the Isle of the Lost for the single goal of eradicating Auradon's heroes. They're using the Dark Net to draw members and posting incendiary pictures of us to fire up hostile sentiment. To the villains on the island, we're basically traitors. They're using what happened at the Coronation to gather numbers on their side, and when they're ready, they'll come for Auradon."

The room went silent at Carlos's words.

"But, um, it's just a theory," said Carlos, to try to lighten up the vibe.

"What's that?" asked Mal, pointing to the small type underneath each picture: *#AntiHeroesUnite #IRL #CAW #Yadrutas #2359 #BeThere.*

"I was about to get to that," said Carlos. "I cracked the code. I think it's a meeting invitation. 'IRL' is short for 'in real life,' which means it's taking place in the real world, not the online world. 'CAW' was harder, but I think it's the location."

"C-A-W?" asked Evie. "But that's—"

"The Castle Across the Way, your house, yep," said Carlos. "It looks like that's where it's being held."

"But what's . . . Yadrutas?" said Mal, frowning as she tried to pronounce the strange word.

"That one took me a while, but after staring at the word for an hour, I realized there was something familiar about it. It's Saturday, spelled backward! And two-three-five-nine is 23:59 in knight time, or 11:59 at night in royal time. So just before midnight this Saturday, there will be an Anti-Heroes meeting at the Castle Across the Way. 'Be there' is obvious. They're telling their members to be there."

"You think?" teased Evie.

"Saturday night, right before midnight. Hold on," said Mal. She grabbed a book from behind her desk. "It's a moon calendar; I was using it to try to figure out what the notes were saying about the moon. Look at this—the end of the old moon, or moonset, is on Friday before midnight, and the new moon rises on Saturday at 11:59. The young moon is Sunday, which is too late. I think the notes are connected to this Anti-Heroes club. Someone wants us to go to this meeting."

"So we were right," said Evie. "Evil Queen, Jafar, Cruella, and Maleficent are behind it somehow. Mal said her mom goes by moon dates."

"You guys really think it's them?" asked Carlos quietly. He had gone a bit pale again, thinking of having to face his mother. He wouldn't be able to hide behind a computer or an invention this time, and he truly wasn't looking forward to going back to being her much-maligned personal servant. He was just starting to enjoy a life that didn't revolve around fluffing furs and fixing wigs.

"Yeah, they must have sent those messages to tell us to go back to the island so they can humiliate us at this Anti-Heroes thing, don't you think?" said Evie.

"I love how they're using our 'bad example' to recruit members while also telling us to go back and join them," said Mal.

"That sounds exactly like something they would do," said Carlos. "They probably have something awful planned for our homecoming." He shivered at the thought.

"Plus, who else would be planning a meeting in Evil Queen's castle?" said Mal. "It has to be them."

"True. And Evil Queen probably took Maleficent's spot the second she swooped off the Isle," said Carlos thoughtfully. "You know they fought over who would get to lead the

Isle of the Lost when they were first banished there."

"They sure did," said Evie. "And that's why we were exiled to the Castle Across the Way!"

"Actually, you didn't invite me to your birthday party, and *that's* why you guys had to move," reminded Mal. "I was only six years old."

"That wasn't my fault," Evie protested. "And you almost let me fall asleep for a thousand years!"

"What's past is past, let bygones be bygones," said Jay, entering the room. "What else did I miss?"

Mal nodded. "Jay's right; sorry, Evie."

"I'm sorry too," said Evie. She stared at the screen again, at the giant red *X*s written across their faces. Ugh, red did not look good on her complexion.

Carlos brought Jay up to speed on what they'd discovered so far about the Anti-Heroes group on the Dark Net. They looked at the picture again.

"We need to be at that meeting so we can find out what they're planning, and that way we can stop it like we did last time," Mal said, a serious look on her face.

"Fine, let's go, I'll start packing," said Carlos, who was dreading it but wanted to get it over as quickly as possible. Like ripping off a Band-Aid. It would be easier to confront his mother sooner rather than later, before he had a change of heart.

"Hold on," said Jay. "Not so fast. Let's think it through. You know what Fairy Godmother always says."

"Don't run in glass slippers?" joked Evie.

"Look before you leap, the slow turtle always wins the race," said Jay. "Oh, and it's always best to be home before midnight."

chapter

Plans Within Plans

Jay smiled at his friends and rubbed his palms. He loved when a plan started to come together. It reminded him of his life back on the Isle, when he would figure out the best way to nab the least rotten banana from the fruit stands. "We can't leave just yet," he repeated.

"Why not?" Carlos wanted to know, even though he looked relieved to hear they didn't have to sneak out of town right then.

"For one, you and I have a tourney game on Saturday, and we can't let the team down," he said. "If Ben doesn't make it back from wherever he is, and we leave, they're down three starters; there's no way they have a chance against the Lost

Boys. They need us." He looked meaningfully at Carlos. "I know you weren't at practice today, but we're counting on you to be ready by game time."

Carlos sighed. "Right."

Jay turned to Mal and Evie, who both looked skeptical. "You guys understand, we're part of something bigger here than just us. We're part of Auradon now," he told them. "You know we are."

"Yes, but—" Mal tried to argue.

"Besides," he interrupted with an apologetic smile. "We don't want this Anti-Heroes group to think we're onto them. What do you think will happen if news gets out that the four of us are suddenly missing from school? We need to go back, but on our own terms. We can't let them know we know."

Mal considered it for a moment, thinking. Finally she nodded. "Okay. Jay's right. We need to lie low," she said. "We'll leave Saturday after the game since everyone gets off-campus privileges on the weekend. Come back Sunday night like everyone else, be back here in time for class on Monday."

"Now you're talking." Jay smiled.

"Wait, hold on," said Evie. "If Jay and Carlos get to play tourney, what about the dance? I'm part of the royal committee, and I have to make sure everything's set up correctly. Otherwise, what if it looks like Wonderland threw up on everything? Plus, it's right after the game, and people will notice if we're not there, especially you, Mal. Even if Ben's not there, people will be expecting you."

"So we go to the dance too," agreed Jay. "Why not?"

Carlos made a few calculations in his head. "The game ends by five, and the dance starts at six, we stay for an hour, maybe, to make sure everyone notices that we were there. That doesn't leave us a whole lot of time to get out of here and to the Isle by midnight, but it's doable."

"And this way you guys won't let down your team," said Evie.

"And Evie gets to set up with her committee," added Jay.

"And Mal gets to . . . dance?" said Carlos.

"We all get to dance," said Evie, whose eyes were sparkling now.

Mal threw up her hands. "Okay," she said. "We won't leave till after the game and the dance so we don't arouse suspicion, and I guess it's good to live up to our responsibilities."

They discussed the logistics of their plan for sneaking out of Auradon: Evie would come up with disguises while Jay would figure out transportation.

"Did we miss anything?" Mal asked.

"Yes, I think so," said Carlos after a moment. "So far the plan can get us out of here, but wouldn't people notice that we're gone on Sunday? That would raise some alarms, don't you think? Even though we're allowed to be off campus for the weekend, people might think it's strange since we never go anywhere."

"Oh, right," said Jay with a sheepish smile. "What are we going to do about that?"

Mal grimaced, thinking hard. "We're going to be gone for less than twenty-four hours. How about we all pretend to catch some sort of bug that keeps us in our rooms, and we can post things online about how sick we are, when in reality we're actually running around the island. Isn't that what our online feeds are for? To convince people you're doing something that you're not?"

"I don't think that's what they're for, actually," said Carlos.

"No, it's perfect," said Jay. "We all get the flu. No one will want to be near us, then. Everyone will leave us alone."

"Evie, can you set up our accounts so that the posts show up automatically? We won't be able to update them ourselves from the Isle," Mal pointed out.

"Of course," said Evie. "I feel like I've been training my whole life for this." She batted her eyelashes jokingly before looking serious again. "So we're taking off on Saturday night for sure?"

"For sure," said Carlos, who had turned a bit green. "What are you smiling about?" he snapped at Jay, who was leaning back, arms behind his head, looking like he hadn't a care in the world. "Aren't you scared?"

"Totally, but I sort of expected something like this would happen," Jay replied.

"What do you mean you expected something like this

to happen?" demanded Carlos, who was practically pulling out his black-and-white hair at the roots at the thought of returning home so soon.

"I just did," Jay said, and stopped to consider why he felt that way. He had grown up on the Isle of the Lost, scrounged for food in the garbage, survived goblin-made coffee, and his favorite snack was still stale popcorn. Even after living in Auradon, he would always be a bit skeptical of happily-ever-after. And honestly, he'd been waiting for the other shoe to drop ever since the Coronation.

"I don't know, because it can't be this easy, right? We win one battle against Maleficent and it's over?" he told them. "No way; haven't we learned by now that there are always monsters hiding under beds, or in the closet, or, um, escaping from island prisons? Monsters who are related to us even."

"You think our parents are monsters?" Evie asked, her voice faint.

"Well, we all know mine certainly is," said Mal. "Fire-breathing dragon and everything."

They all laughed. But Jay was still thinking of what he'd said about their parents. *Was* Jafar a monster? Jafar might take things to the extreme, but he was also just Jay's slightly overweight, pajama-wearing dad, who dreamt of gold and riches beyond his wildest imagination. A man driven by greed who thought only of himself wasn't much of a monster on an island without magic. But what would happen if

Jafar was able to get his magic back? Like Maleficent, Jafar had a powerful magical staff, a cobra that could hypnotize and manipulate those who came under its thrall. Who knew what he would be capable of doing then? But Jay already knew that answer. It's what had landed his father in the Isle of the Lost in the first place.

So no, Jay wasn't surprised that their parents were up to something new, and while he was frightened, he also knew that it didn't matter if all of them were scared. If it was true that this Anti-Heroes movement was growing on the Isle of the Lost, and that their errant parents—Jafar, Evil Queen, and Cruella de Vil—were behind it, he and his friends were the only ones who could stop them. "As Mal said herself, Maleficent is definitely a monster, but we took care of Maleficent, didn't we?" he said. "So we can handle this, whatever it is."

"But what if Maleficent is part of it too?" said Evie worriedly. "What if she's not completely harmless like we think she is?"

"Maleficent almost roasted us all alive," Carlos reminded them.

"And who knows what my mom, Jafar, and Cruella have in store for us," said Evie. "I'm not sure I really want to find out."

"Come on, guys. We can handle anything. We can handle Maleficent," Jay said staunchly. "Right, Mal?" He elbowed their fearless leader.

Mal elbowed Jay back, almost a shove. She was clearly just as terrified as the rest of them, but she had decided, like Jay, to keep it under control. "Yes, of course, Jay's right. We can handle this. We *will* handle this." She took a deep breath and stuck out her hand, motioning to the others to do the same. One by one they each put a hand on top of hers.

"For Auradon," she said.

"For Auradon," said Jay, slapping his hand down.

"For Auradon," whispered Evie, adding hers gently.

They all turned to Carlos, waiting.

"For Auradon," he said finally, and very reluctantly put his hand on top.

It was done. They were afraid of their parents, but they would move forward regardless. Mal always pulled them together, and Jay could feel the relief that now filled the room.

chapter 10

Energy = Magic Squared?

Jay's plan for getting them transportation back to the island was simple. They would leave Auradon as they entered it, in the royal limousine, which also held the remote control that opened the invisible dome and let down the connecting bridge with a click of a button.

But if the four villain kids were going to leave Auradon Prep without being noticed, then they couldn't leave looking like themselves; that much was clear. They didn't have family or friends in the other kingdoms, so there was no reason for them to leave school before winter break. They would have to be creative. Thankfully, being creative was not a problem for Evie.

"Leave that to me," she'd told the team the night before. "I've got this handled. If you get the wheels, Jay, I'll make sure no one knows it's us in the royal limousine."

But for now, she still had time for regular life. After class, Evie headed to the grand ballroom, where tomorrow's Castlecoming dance would be held, for the last planning meeting. The annual tourney game and dance was a traditional affair, celebrating school alumni returning to their old stomping grounds, when good ol' princes and princesses regaled everyone with tales of the pranks pulled back in their day—stealing the Auradon mascot, for instance, or the time they glued the classroom furniture to the ceiling, causing Fairy Godmother to exclaim something a little more colorful than "Bibbidi-Bobbidi-Boo!"

Evie said hello to the fellow members of the dance committee and the meeting began. Since the dance was so close, almost all the details had already been agreed upon. The menu had been approved, and Mr. and Mrs. Darling had volunteered to chaperone along with Roger and Anita Radcliffe. Lonnie was going to be the DJ, and would be bringing her own equipment. All that was left was to decide on a theme for the decorations.

"We could do an imperial banquet?" suggested Lonnie.

"How about a sultan's feast?" asked Jordan. "We could tent the whole area!"

No one seemed to like any of those ideas, least of all Evie, who argued that since it was Castlecoming, the theme of the decorations should reflect the school colors—royal blue and gold.

"Yes, you have a point there," said Audrey. "But don't you think pale pink and baby blue are so much prettier?"

"It's not a baby shower," Evie mumbled under her breath.

"I'm sorry, did you say something?" asked Audrey, pretending not to have heard.

"I agree with Evie," said Allie. "But can we do something more psychedelic maybe? In Wonderland, we have the most amazing flowers of so many different hues."

"Mmm," said Evie, looking around at the lush, cream-colored carpet and exquisite Auradon Prep tapestries already hung on the ballroom's walls. "Both sound lovely, but I do think blue and gold would be best. It fits the existing color scheme in the room."

"If you say so." Allie sighed. "I suppose that is traditional."

"So we'll go with a gold balloon banner? And blue velvet ribbons around all the columns?" said Evie, pen poised at the ready.

"Maybe we can have bunches of violets in gold vases?" said Allie. "Violets are actually blue."

"Perfect!" She smiled at Allie.

"And we can trim the tables with gold leaf," said Lonnie helpfully.

Audrey frowned. "If you guys really think that's best."

Evie smiled. She knew when she had won, and she could be gracious in victory. "Audrey, Lonnie, do you want to come over and try on your ball gowns?" she asked. "I'm pretty much done with them."

If Mal was famous for helping with hair, Evie's talents as a fashion designer and seamstress were starting to become legendary. A number of girls had asked if she would make dresses for them for the dance, so when Mal had said they would need to leave Auradon undercover, it had given Evie an idea.

"Ooh, I can't wait!" said Audrey. "Did you put on the swan bustle like I asked?"

"It was difficult, but I did it," said Evie with a smile.

"I can't wait to see mine!" said Lonnie. "Is it red and gold like we talked about?"

"You'll look like an empress," Evie promised.

The girls followed her back to her room and Evie handed them their gowns. There was much oohing and aahing over the gorgeous dresses. Audrey's gown featured pink and blue panels that changed color depending on how she twirled her skirt. "It's like magic!" Audrey sighed, unable to keep her eyes off her reflection.

"I think Cinderella's mice are going to be jealous!" said Lonnie, who looked stunning in a traditional imperial column with a pretty lotus print. "Mary's definitely going to want to hire you when you graduate from here."

"Thanks, guys," said Evie with a smile.

After they'd changed back into their school clothes, Audrey wandered over to Evie's vanity table, which was littered with numerous tiny glass pots filled with different colors. She stuck her finger in one. "What's this?"

"Oh, just some batches of lip gloss I've been experimenting with in the lab. We always had to use expired cosmetics on the Isle of the Lost, so when I got here and discovered I could learn to make my own makeup, I was thrilled. I've even been able to enhance them with the right chemical compounds," said Evie. "Look, here's one that changes from pink to blue in the light."

Audrey squealed. "Can I have it?"

"It's yours," said Evie.

Lonnie held up a clear gloss. "What does this do?"

"Glows in the dark," said Evie. "I thought it would be fun when the lights go down during the dance."

"Cool," said Lonnie. They crowded around the vanity, picking up tubes and pots and trying every color. Lonnie held up a purple one. "And this?"

"Don't you hate when your lip gloss disappears in the middle of the day? So I figured out how to make one that never fades," said Evie.

Lonnie and Audrey nodded in agreement.

"Are you sure I can have this one?" asked Audrey, holding up her blue-pink pot.

"I made it for you, of course," said Evie. "Which one do you want, Lonnie?"

"The glow-in-the-dark one, thanks. That way everyone can see me smiling up in the DJ booth," said Lonnie.

"Perfect."

The girls thanked Evie and left with their dresses. Mal walked in a few minutes later. "All set?" she asked.

In answer, Evie opened the closet door, which held two identical dresses to the ones she had made for Audrey and Lonnie. "Try yours on," she said. "I want to see if it fits."

Evie had stayed up way too late the night before, but she'd gotten them done. If they were going to leave Auradon, they would do so disguised as princesses. Lonnie and Audrey often left school to visit their home castles and kingdoms, and no one would question their use of the royal limousine. Jay and Carlos would be dressed as their chauffeur and bodyguard, respectively.

"How's your mom, by the way?" asked Evie as she zipped Mal up into the replica of Audrey's dress. "Did she tell you anything the other day?"

Mal shook her head. "Not unless she was communicating by sleeping. I really don't see how it could be her, but who knows. We'll just have to assume the worst." She caught her reflection. Her purple hair framed her horrified face as the dress shimmered in waves of sparkly pink and blue. "Oh, my goblins, I look like such a princess! It's so . . . pink . . . and blue!"

Evie laughed. "That's the point! Though I have to say, these *really* aren't your colors."

Mal stuck her tongue out at Evie. "Any luck with the Magic Mirror?"

"None," said Evie. "It works perfectly if I ask it to show me anything else. But if I ask to see my mom, Jafar, or Cruella, it's just cloudy. It's like they've disappeared or something."

"Let me see," said Mal. "Do you think there might be a crack in it?"

"It's already cracked," said Evie.

"Maybe I can try a spell or two." Mal grabbed her spell book from the shelf, the one that Maleficent had passed down to her. "Magic Mirror at my command, heal thyself with my own hand!"

The mirror remained the same.

"Magic Mirror, do as I say, show us the villains on the Isle today!" said Mal.

Nothing changed. Evie shook her head. "I don't think there's anything wrong with the mirror at all. I'm starting to believe they don't want to be found. They're able to hide from it somehow."

"But the only way to do that is with magic," said Mal. "And there's no magic on the Isle."

"Or maybe the Magic Mirror is weakening," said Evie thoughtfully. "Since we're not encouraged to do magic here, I haven't been using it as much."

"What of it?"

"Well, what if magic is like a muscle: if you don't use it, it atrophies or tries to find somewhere else to go. Energy has to transform, right? That's what we learned in chemistry," said Evie. "There's no such thing as turning something into nothing. It just becomes something else, even if we don't see it."

Mal considered this. "You know, you might be right."

chapter 11

A Wish Is a Dream Your Heart Makes

The biggest barrier—literally and figuratively—in their plan to return to the Isle of the Lost was the invisible dome that covered the island. There was no way in or out of the island without the king's permission. Of course, it would have been easy enough to ask for Ben's help, except he was out of town. Also Mal didn't want the king to have to answer to his councillors and his subjects if they learned he'd allowed four villain kids to return to the Isle of the Lost now that the borders were guarded more rigorously than ever after Maleficent's attack. The recent embargo meant most of the goblin barges that brought in supplies and leftovers to the Isle had been blocked, and the few that were allowed through were being monitored very closely.

Hence Jay had decided on stealing the royal limousine for their escape. The only problem was how to get hold of the car without being caught.

Luckily, the one person who could help him had already issued an invitation. Jordan had asked him to stop by her lamp that afternoon. She was recording a new episode of her popular online show and planned to interview him as one of Auradon's Top Tourney players in the lead-up to the Castlecoming game that weekend.

Jay followed her directions to the lamp, which was kept on a special shelf in the residence halls. Jordan's lamp was smaller than her father's, made of rose gold with delicate filigree carvings all over its surface. Jay wondered if he should pick it up and decided not to. Instead he called down into the lamp's spout. "Hello in there! Jordan?"

"Just rub the front and you'll pop in," he heard Jordan yell from inside. "No need to shout! I can hear you loud and clear!"

He did as told and soon found himself comfortably seated on a pink velvet footstool across from a small octagonal coffee table. Green columns painted with gold swirls circled the spacious room, and heavy blue curtains draped dramatically from the ceiling. A striking purple-and-gold Oriental rug was centered on the floor, and peacock feathers were arranged in vases all around. "Neat," he said. "It's bigger than it looks."

"Thanks, I like my space," said Jordan, who was seated across from him on a purple footstool.

"Is it annoying that this is all the magic you can use at school?" Jay asked, picking up one of the many stuffed pillows.

"Not really," said Jordan. "I'm actually glad for the restrictions. Magic can be wildly unpredictable, so even though it's fun, it's nice to have a break from it sometimes."

"So no more granting wishes, huh?" he teased.

"Not today, anyway," she said cheerfully. "Ready for your interview?"

"Hit me," Jay said.

Jordan snapped her fingers and the lights went on. "Welcome to *TourneyCenter*!" she said, smiling into the camera. "Today we have Jay, a star player on Auradon's Knights! Jay, so glad you could join us!"

"Great to be here, Jordan."

"Are you excited about the upcoming game? Do you think the team is ready to win the tournament?" she asked.

"Very excited, and I think we're more than ready."

"The Lost Boys have a killer defense; how do you think the Knights will succeed?"

"The way we always do: we run hard, we dodge the cannons, we make the goals."

"You're confident."

"I am, I know our team."

"What about the rumors that King Ben won't be back in time to play the game? We've heard he left earlier this week on some secret official business," Jordan said keenly. "Can you tell us anything about that?"

"I can't speak to the rumors, but I know Ben wouldn't want to let us down. I hope he makes it back in time, but if not, we'll carry on."

"I'm sure you will," she said, rifling through her index cards for the next question. She smiled back up at the camera. "One of the things we like to do on *TourneyCenter* is to get to know our players better. Can you tell us a little about yourself?"

"Well, I'm Jay, son of Jafar. I grew up on the Isle of the Lost, but I think everyone knows that by now."

"That's right, you're one of the so-called villain kids. When did you move here?" she asked.

Jay perked up at the question. "At the start of the school year. A big old limousine picked us up and dropped us off at Auradon Prep's front door."

"How fancy," said Jordan, leaning forward with a smile.

"Sure was. The amount of candy they have in the back of that thing, I've got to tell you, Jordan, I wish I had the keys to that limo in my pocket right now," he said, rubbing his stomach.

"Jay! You know the rules!" Jordan said, looking worried. "You can't say the word *wish* in my lamp. Otherwise . . .

Check your pocket for the keys. You'll have to return . . ." She trailed off as the entire room went topsy-turvy, and the two of them were thrown across the lamp like rag dolls.

"Must have been another earthquake," said Jordan, struggling to right herself and her footstool. Lamps had crashed, pillows and peacock feathers were scattered everywhere. "They're so annoying! Every time one hits, my lamp falls on the floor. When you leave would you mind putting it back on the shelf?"

"Not at all," said Jay with a smile, noticing she had forgotten all about the limousine keys. He felt guilty for deliberately deceiving Jordan, and tricking her into using her magic. But since it was for a good cause, maybe that was okay? The villain kids were just trying to protect Auradon from harm. He'd have to ask Fairy Godmother about it next time in Remedial Goodness class.

Jordan wrapped up the interview and thanked him for stopping by.

As Jay walked back toward campus, the keys to the royal limousine jingled in his pocket.

chapter 12

Castlecoming Queens

Saturday morning dawned bright and early, and Mal woke up with the sun. She'd been unable to sleep the night before, thinking about the day to come. Tonight they would return to the Isle of the Lost to confront this sinister Anti-Heroes organization most likely headed up by the biggest villains in the land. *We can do this; we have to,* she thought to herself, but a small, worried part of her was anxious just the same.

"I'm terrified too," Evie said, when she saw the look on Mal's face as they got ready for the day. "But like you said, we can handle it."

"I think Jay said that."

"Yes, but we all know you're the one who's going to make it happen," Evie said confidently. "And if you don't, well, at least your lip gloss won't fade." She handed Mal a jar full of a purple tint. "You know what my mom always says, beauty is as beauty is."

Mal smiled at Evie and Evie smiled at Mal. It was wonderful to have supportive friends, especially when they were good at conjuring up cosmetics. Mal carefully applied the gloss, liking the way it matched her purple varsity jacket. She told Evie she'd meet her at the game and headed over to the library to check on Maleficent one last time before they left.

Her mother was curled around a rock. She looked so tiny and helpless that it was hard to imagine how she could have anything to do with the mischief that was going down on the Isle. "If there's anything you want to say to me, if you can change back, you should let me know, Mom," she told the tiny lizard.

But Maleficent just kept sleeping on her warm rock.

"Fine," said Mal. "I'll see you when I get back."

She left the library and walked to breakfast. The entire campus was festooned with balloons and banners, a lively feeling in the air as students walked around with their parents. She saw Audrey with her mother, Aurora, poring over the class pictures that hung in the hallways. Doug was taking a family of dwarfs on a prospective students' tour. "This is where we have choir practice. I'm sure your kids will love singing in it," Mal overheard him say proudly.

For a brief moment, Mal wished she could be one of those kids showing off the school to their parents, but Maleficent had never even once attended a villain–teacher conference back at Dragon Hall, and it was futile to think she would find anything to admire about Auradon Prep.

But she didn't have time to worry about feeling out of place on Castlecoming day. Friendly students mobbed her, eager to introduce her to their parents.

"Come meet my parents!" said Lonnie, introducing her to Mulan and Li Shang.

"Mother, this is Mal! I told you all about her!" said Allie, who pulled Alice away from admiring the students' artwork displayed on the walls.

Mal shook so many hands and smiled so much her dimples were starting to hurt. People in Auradon were so nice, it was a little exhausting. She wished Ben were back already. He was still out of town, and he'd let her know he was sorry, but he wouldn't make it back in time for the tourney game or the dance after all. Mal was surprised to find that she was actually quite disappointed about it, but at least she and Evie would still have fun. Mal would never admit it out loud, but dancing with her friends was nearly as good as going on a date with the King of Auradon.

"Mal, over here!" Evie called from the other end of the hall. Mal joined her side and they walked together to the tourney stadium. The band was already playing the Auradon fight song as they found their seats.

Evie handed her a piece of white silk.

"What's this for?" Mal asked, noticing that everyone else in the nearby crowd had one. The stands on the Auradon side were full of people holding the white silk streamers, waving them gaily about.

"To cheer on our knights, duh," replied Evie, waving hers.

Mal inspected it closely. "Hankies?"

"It's what ladies used to wave at their knights, you know, back when they had real tourneys, with horses. They used to call it 'waving their colors.' Don't you remember? We learned it in class."

The Royal History of Auradon, Mal recalled now. She waved her white hankie, though really, this practice probably should have stayed behind in the Middle Ages. The crowd cheered when the Auradon Knights took the field; Mal and Evie hooted loudly when Jay and Carlos were introduced.

Carlos waved, smiling behind his helmet, and Jay gave them a thumbs-up. Chad was nowhere in the starting lineup and pouted from the bench.

The game was a close one. Without Ben to help Jay with the tourney plays, the Lost Boys nearly defeated the Knights on their home turf, but in the end Jay set up Carlos for the winning score, and the stands exploded in celebration.

"I'm glad we decided to stay for the game," Mal told Evie. "Jay was right, we needed to be here."

The girls went back to their rooms to change into their dresses for the dance. "Remember, we're only staying for a little bit, then we leave and change into Lonnie's and Audrey's gowns, and meet the boys in the parking lot," said Mal as she fluffed up her lavender skirts in the mirror. The dress had just enough volume without being fussy, and the dark leather cap sleeves were embellished with tiny black crystals, which meant they shimmered in the light but didn't look princessy.

"Right," said Evie, sounding doubtful.

"Evie!" Mal said. "What's the matter? This is the plan."

"But let's not go so soon, okay? Can't we have a little fun at least?" she wheedled, until Mal had to agree. "I promised Doug we'd dance the Heigh-Ho Slide."

"Does he know about our plan?" Mal asked. She hadn't forbidden the group to tell anyone, but had assumed they wouldn't.

"No, I didn't tell him. I don't want him to have to lie for me." Evie straightened her tiara and took a deep breath. "Plus, I don't want him to worry. As far as he'll know, I'll be leaving the dance with a bad stomachache and then I'll be in my room with the flu all weekend like we agreed."

"I'm sorry we have to go so soon," said Mal. "I know how much you love dances. You really do look like—"

"The Fairest?" asked Evie with a cheeky grin.

"Let's just say every princess at that dance is definitely safe from a huntsman tonight," said Mal.

"Okay, let's do this," said Evie. They linked arms and headed out the door.

The ballroom was festooned with so many balloons that it was hard to see the top of the ceiling. Gold bunting and blue ribbons hung everywhere.

"It's perfect." Evie sighed.

"That is a whole lot of balloons," Mal said.

"You think? I was worried it wouldn't be enough," said Evie. "I doubled the order."

They waved to Lonnie, who was manning the turntables up at the DJ booth. The Auradon tourney team trooped in, handsome in their formal wear, and Jay and Carlos found them, exuberant and smiling. They were the stars of the evening, surrounded by a group of admiring friends and teammates, while Chad skulked by the punch. Evie left to dance with Doug, and Jay and Carlos headed for the buffet tables. Mal picked at her food and checked the clock. She was impatient to get going and was relieved when it was finally time to gather up her team.

She elbowed Jay, and he reluctantly put down the plate of desserts he was holding.

"Let's go," she said. "I'll grab Evie, you get Carlos, and we'll meet you at the car."

Mal felt her stomach flip as they set their plan in motion. Sure, she had faced down Maleficent and won once before. But who knew what kind of darkness awaited them this time? Alas, there was only one way to find out.

chapter 13

Ticket to Ride

Carlos had never thought of himself as much of a dancer, but during the celebration after Maleficent's defeat, when all of Auradon had danced on the school steps, he'd enjoyed shaking a leg with the group. Who knew he had it in him? And he was enjoying dancing with Jane, who looked pretty with her hair back to its original color and neat style instead of the long, glossy mane Mal's spell had created. Carlos thought Jane's normal hair suited her better. Some people didn't really need makeovers, just more confidence.

He was spinning her around when Jay tapped on his

shoulder. "Uh, I'm headed out," Jay said. "I'm not feeling too well. What about you?"

Carlos was about to say he felt great when he remembered the plan. "Right! I, uh, I'm not feeling well either. Sorry, Jane." He clutched his middle and pretended to double up in pain.

"Oh!" she said. "Are you okay?"

"I'm fine, I think I just have to lie down now," he said. "Thanks for the dance."

"No, thank you!" said Jane, a little wistfully.

Carlos crouch-walked out of the ballroom with Jay, who also made a show of looking ill. When they were outside the building, they straightened up and broke into a run toward the parking lot. They could still hear the music wafting from the dance as they made their way noiselessly across campus. They stopped uneasily when the ground rolled beneath them with a little tremor, but it faded away and they kept going.

Jay placed a chauffeur's cap on his head and Carlos stuck in a fake earpiece. Since they were both already wearing black suits, Evie decided that was all they needed to complete the disguise as driver and bodyguard to the royal princesses. Now all they could hope for was that no one who saw them would know that Audrey and Lonnie were still at the dance.

They found the limousine, which had Auradon flags on

each side of the hood. Jay removed the keys from his pocket and unlocked the car doors. He got in on the driver's side and Carlos climbed into the passenger seat.

"Bridge remote?" asked Jay.

"Check," said Carlos. "Found it in the glove compartment."

There was a rustle of skirts from behind them, and the girls appeared out of the darkness. Mal had spelled their hair so that from far away, she and Evie really looked like Audrey and Lonnie. Actually, the disguise was so good that Carlos almost had a little panic attack thinking the real princesses were headed their way.

Mal opened the back door and they climbed in. "Hurry," she said. "We need to get there before midnight."

"Your chariot awaits, my ladies," joked Jay, who revved up the engine.

"Um, Jay? Where did you learn to drive?" Evie asked, peeking out from the partition that separated the front of the car from the back.

"Street rats!" Jay cursed, hitting the steering wheel in frustration. "I was hoping you'd forget that I don't, technically, know how."

"Oh, for fur's sake," said Carlos. "Switch places."

"Carlos, *you* know how to drive?" asked Mal, impressed. "How?"

"I taught myself," Carlos said. "My mom has a car, remember? She would make me drive her to the Queen of

Hearts's salon all the time." He placed the chauffeur's cap on his head and handed Jay the earpiece.

"Thank goodness!" said Evie.

"I don't think goodness had anything to do with it, actually," said Carlos with a smile. He eased the long car out of the parking lot. "Hey, if there's any candy back there, you guys have to share."

Mal threw him a huge lollipop that bonked him on the head, and they were off.

chapter 14

My Boyfriend's Back

They had only traveled a few feet and hadn't even left the school grounds when a flood of light covered the darkened driveway, and the limousine had to stop in its tracks. Mal squinted against the light to try to see who was blocking their way.

"It's the royal carriage!" said Evie. "Ben must be back!"

"What do we do now?" said Carlos nervously. "I can't go around it, it's too big."

The royal carriage was an imposing behemoth, resembling not so much a pumpkin as a giant squash on wheels. A footman opened the door and Ben stepped out, shaded his eyes against the light, and peered into the limousine.

Carlos switched off the ignition, resigned. "Oh, well, looks like we're not going anywhere now," he said, trying to sound disappointed, and failing.

"Let me handle it," said Mal, stepping out of the car to meet Ben.

"Audrey?" Ben asked, when he saw her.

"No, uh, it's me, Mal," she said, feeling shy and a bit silly at the whole getup and embarrassed that they'd been caught sneaking out of Auradon. After all their careful planning, this was a bit anticlimactic.

"Mal?" He gaped. "What's going on? What are you wearing? Is that a dress of Audrey's? It's so pink and blue. And is that the royal limousine?"

The windows rolled down, and the rest of the group waved cheerfully at Ben. Ben waved back, a bit confused. "Why does Evie look like Lonnie and why is Carlos driving? Does he even have a license?"

"I can explain," said Mal. She quickly told him about the mysterious messages they'd received, the Anti-Heroes thread on the Dark Net, and the missing villains.

Ben listened carefully, rocking back and forth on his heels, taking it all in. "So now you're all headed back to the Isle of the Lost?"

Mal nodded. "We have to, we have to see what's going on."

"I see." He wasn't frowning, which was a good sign, but he wasn't smiling either. "And you weren't going to tell me; why?"

"We didn't want to get you in trouble—with your subjects, I mean," said Mal. "Everyone's a little nervous ever since the Coronation, and we didn't think it would look good for you if you knew we were going back to the Isle of the Lost, especially with the embargo and all."

"Hmm," said Ben. "Okay."

"Okay?" asked Mal. "You're not mad?"

"No, why should I be? You're not doing anything wrong . . . well, except maybe Jay shouldn't have tricked Jordan out of the keys, you and Evie shouldn't be pretending to be Audrey and Lonnie, and Carlos shouldn't be driving without a license," he said mildly, but he had a hint of a smile on his face.

"But you're not going to stop us?" asked Mal.

"No. You guys should definitely check out what's happening back there. I don't know if I would have agreed to it if you'd asked me beforehand, but now that I do know about it, I think it's the right thing to do," he said. "Tell Carlos to send me the link to the Dark Net, and I'll keep an eye on this Anti-Heroes thread in case it looks like you might need backup."

"Definitely. And we'll be back in time for class on Monday," she told him. "We just wanted to check it out. Although if something is going down, we might be delayed longer. But I don't want you to worry."

"I won't. I know you can watch out for yourself," he said, taking her hand. "I'm glad I caught you, though. I wanted to tell you, strange things are happening, and not just on the Isle of the Lost. In Auradon too."

"You mean like the earthquakes?" she asked.

He raised his eyebrows. "Not just the earthquakes, but lately there have been unseasonal hurricanes down by the Bayou, and giant sandstorms in Agrabah too."

"What do they think is causing it?" she asked.

"We don't know yet. But that's not all." He hesitated.

"What is it? Where were you, by the way? What's wrong?" she asked, his somber expression making her feel anxious.

"Camelot Heights," he said. "It's why I took the carriage; their roads are hard on cars over there. Merlin came to the council with Artie on Monday, to ask for help with a strange creature that was attacking their town."

"What kind of creature?" Mal asked, dreading the answer already. "What kind of attacks?"

Ben held her gaze. "One that was burning forests, stealing livestock, and scorching farms. A real menace," he said. "Everyone's really scared. All of Camelot Heights is under lockdown right now."

"Oh no," she said. "That's awful."

"Mal, it was a purple dragon," he said quietly, letting the words sink in. He told her about how he had set up camp with Camelot's knights on the edge of the forest and waited for days for the creature to appear. "Artie was on watch that night and woke us all up. It came out of nowhere, but I saw it before it vanished. A huge purple dragon, with bright green eyes."

"What. No. You can't think . . ." she said, her heart racing. This was madness. There was only one purple dragon in the world. Maleficent.

"I saw it," he said. "It looked just like her. . . . I'll never forget how she looked during the Coronation. Her face was right in front of mine and she was going to roast me alive, until you stopped her. I'm telling you, it was her."

Mal crossed her arms and kept shaking her head. "No, just no. It can't be. I just saw her this morning. She's trapped under glass on her pedestal. Tiny. Helpless. And you know as well as I do that her Dragon's Eye scepter is safely locked away in the museum. She's powerless and can't wield any magic without it."

"I know what I saw," said Ben, his face drawn. "I know how crazy it sounds. But just in case, I'm going to place more guards in the library, and keep cameras on her 24/7. If she is getting out, we have to know how she's doing it."

"I'm sorry I can't stay here to help you," she said, upset to hear this new information.

Ben smiled. "As much as I'd prefer that, I think it would be the wrong move. I'm going to stay here in Auradon to see if we can track the dragon down before it does more damage. We're keeping it off the news; I don't want to cause a panic. You guys go find out what's going on in the Isle of the Lost. Maybe this is all part of a bigger scheme. Let me know what you find, and don't be afraid to ask for help if you need it."

"I will," she said, giving him a tight hug. "Thanks, Ben."

"Is there anything else you need?" he asked.

"No, I think we're good."

Ben hugged her one more time, then helped her into the car. The windows were still open and the four villain kids waved goodbye, nervous and hopeful expressions on their faces.

"Good luck," Ben told them. "And good game, by the way. Nice work. I caught the highlights on *TourneyCenter*," he said to Jay and Carlos.

"Thanks, man," Carlos called from the driver's seat while Jay bumped fists with Ben through the passenger window.

Ben reached for Mal's hand through her window. "I'll see you on Monday," he said, before reluctantly letting go. He motioned to the carriage driver to get out of the way so the limousine could pass and leave the school gates.

"Monday," she echoed as the car pulled away. Then something occurred to her. "Ben!" she called.

He raised his eyebrows.

"If you do catch the purple dragon . . ." She hesitated, even if she knew Ben of all people, would understand.

"Yes?"

"Don't hurt it, okay?"

He nodded. "You have my word."

Anti-Heroes

"It's up to you how
far you go.
If you don't try,
you'll never know."
—Merlin, The
Sword in the Stone

chapter 15

Isle Sweet Isle

The streets of Auradon were empty as the royal limousine made its way to the very edge of the coast, practically at the shoreline. They finally reached the southernmost point by the bay, where they knew an invisible bridge connecting the island to the mainland was standing. Mal bit the edge of her thumb as she told the rest of her team what Ben had told her about the purple dragon that had been spotted in Camelot. They agreed it had to be impossible—there was no way that creature was her mother. Yet who or what else could it be? There had to be an explanation, but for now, nothing seemed to make sense.

"I sure hope we don't run into this dragon on the Isle,"

said Carlos as he steered the limousine toward the end of the road. The lights from the Isle of the Lost pierced through the fog. "Wow, it actually looks almost pretty from here."

"Home," said Evie softly.

"There's no place like it," said Jay, with forced cheer.

"Let's hope not," said Carlos. "One island full of villains is quite enough."

"Well, what are we waiting for?" said Mal, who knew they had to do this before they all chickened out. "Hit it, Jay."

Jay removed the remote that controlled the bridge from the glove compartment and pointed it at the air in front of them. "Here goes nothing."

There was a spark, and through the haze, Mal could almost see the dome opening up as the bridge slowly manifested before their eyes. Carlos drove the car forward, and the four of them pressed their faces against the windows, watching the bridge materialize in front of them as they drove over the water. Mal knew they were all thinking of the first day they'd left the island. Now they were returning, very much changed from the rotten hellions who had left not too long ago.

Just as they reached the other side, Jay turned around and zapped the remote control again, and the bridge disappeared.

"Don't drive into town," said Mal. "We should hide the car somewhere."

"Good idea," said Carlos, who veered off the main street and into one of the dusty, unfinished roads. But it was hard to steer the large car on such rocky terrain, and Carlos tried to overcompensate by turning the wheel left when he should have turned right, and his passengers screamed as the car swerved and plunged into a ditch, sending everything flying as the limousine crashed into a copse of dead trees.

The engine died and the smoke cleared. "Everyone okay?" Mal called from the backseat. It looked as if their seat belts had saved them from serious injury, and Mal was thankful they had picked up the habit of wearing them in Auradon.

"Sorry, sorry!" said Carlos, coughing from the front.

Evie nodded that she was all right and Jay offered a thumbs-up from the passenger side. "A-OK, except I think we lost the remote to the bridge," he said. "It must have flown out the windshield." He pointed to the huge hole in the middle of the glass.

"We'll just have to find another way to get back," said Mal.

"I guess we could swim?" joked Jay.

"Well, at least the crash took care of one thing. The car's definitely hidden now. No one will find it here," said Carlos.

They took turns changing inside the roomy back passenger area into their normal clothing and began the long walk into town. Mal checked the time. After all of their delays, they still had a few hours before the Anti-Heroes meeting was supposed to start. "Let's meet at Evie's castle a little before midnight," said Mal. "For now, let's split up. Each of you, see if you can locate your parents. Once we know what they're planning, we'll figure out what to do about it."

"What do we say if anyone from the Isle asks why we're back?" asked Evie, looking uncomfortable at the thought.

"Yeah, I bet they're not exactly going to be excited to see us," said Carlos.

"Tell them the truth, that we're visiting our aged relatives," suggested Jay with a grin. Soon they had reached the outskirts of town and passed Dragon Hall, following Woeful Way down to the familiar town square, cornered by shabby buildings on all sides and the Bargain Castle looming over everything.

"Don't let anyone know we know about this Anti-Heroes club," said Mal. "Until we find Cruella, Jafar, and Evil Queen."

The group agreed. "Wow, this place is worse than I remember," said Carlos, looking around. "And what is that smell? Did you guys ever notice that before?" He made a face. "It smells like . . ."

"Poisoned toads," said Mal, who remembered what went into the daily coffee brew.

"Goblins," said Jay, who seemed to have the foul creatures stuck in his mind.

"Garbage," said Evie, who recoiled at the memory.

"Actually, it smells like a combination of all three," Carlos decided.

Mal had to agree, even if a small part of her was happy to return to the familiar "comforts" of home. The outdoor bazaar was closed for the day, but the Slop Shop and Ursula's Fish and Chips were doing brisk business. It was kind of sad to see how terrifically ramshackle everything looked, though. Mal used to revel in dirt and decay, but she'd been in Auradon too long, and now everything was grimier than she remembered. She really needed to chug a cup of toad coffee before she got too soft.

"Look at that," said Jay, pointing to a poster of Maleficent pasted to the side of a wall. Someone had drawn a mustache on her face, and another person had scrawled MISTRESS OF LIZARDS over her forehead.

"Whoa," said Carlos.

"You said it," said Evie. "I guess they saw the Coronation; it was broadcast live to the whole kingdom, even here."

When Maleficent was, well, Maleficent, no one would dare even *think* to vandalize her likeness. There were other changes too. Goblins seemed to have taken over the square. There were dozens and dozens of them, living in cardboard boxes and gathered around little trash-can fires.

"Where did they all come from?" wondered Evie, who had never seen so many.

"The Forbidden Fortress maybe?" Jay guessed. During

their quest for the Dragon's Eye scepter, they had run into a rather large and unfriendly goblin horde.

"Nope," grunted a goblin when he overheard their conversation. He was a stout, runty fellow, and looked as if he hadn't had a good meal in a long while. His green skin was sallow, and his yellow eyes red-rimmed. "We used to work the barges, but with the embargo, there's a limit on how many of us can bring in supplies from the mainland anymore. Maleficent promised us freedom and a better life, but she got turned into a lizard, so here we are."

"Sorry about that," said Mal.

"You the one that did that to her?" the goblin asked.

"Sort of," she replied as Evie pulled her away.

"Didn't your mother ever teach you not to talk to strange goblins?" her friend scolded.

"Of course not," said Mal.

"Mine didn't either," admitted Evie.

They walked through the streets, feeling the eyes of the island's citizens following them. Mal realized that even if they were dressed casually, they were still better dressed and much cleaner-looking than anyone else. Their clothes, unlike their former neighbors' wardrobes, weren't patched and frayed, or ill-fitting and holey. Mal felt a new wave of emotions—a little proud, a little bittersweet, a little abashed that they looked so different from everyone else. And a little scared to think what their old neighbors now thought of them. Did the people of the island now despise them like they did the fancy princes and princesses of Auradon?

In Auradon, people stared at them because they came from somewhere else, and now on the Isle of the Lost, everyone stared at them because they'd left. In a way, it was just the same. Now they were outsiders in both places. Some of the townsfolk looked at them balefully, while others were merely curious.

"Hi, Gaston, and, um, Gaston," said Evie, seeing the burly duo across the street.

But the Gastons simply scowled.

Evie backed away. "They used to be pretty friendly back in Dragon Hall," she said. "They even offered to share their lunch with me."

"Not anymore," said Mal. "I bet they don't even share a crumb with you at this point."

"Let's keep going," urged Carlos. "Everyone's staring. I feel like they'll start throwing rotten tomatoes at us."

"Wouldn't be the first time," said Jay, but he looked nervous too.

"Well, well, if isn't the heroes of Auradon." The four of them turned at the sound of the voice and saw a girl with dark frizzy hair leaning over a balcony. She had piercing gray eyes and wore a soiled red dress with tattered golden piping at the neckline.

"There's that word again," Evie whispered. *"Heroes."*

"Ginny Gothel!" said Mal. "Get down here!" Ginny had been a friendly acquaintance back in Dragon Hall, and Mal remembered with a hint of shame that they had often enjoyed making fun of smaller, weaker people together. They watched as Ginny shimmied down the edge of the building and walked toward them.

Mal wasn't sure what she was expecting when she returned to the Isle of the Lost, but it certainly wasn't to find Ginny Gothel, of all people, looking down at her.

"Don't you guys clean up nice," Ginny sneered, crossing her arms and studying each of them in turn. "What do you call that?" she asked, pointing at Mal's outfit.

Mal flushed. "Preppie punk," she explained. She was wearing a purple argyle sweater underneath her favorite jacket, along with a clean denim skirt and boots.

"Huh. I'm not sure I'm a fan, but then Auradon style is best for goody-goodies. So, what are you guys doing back here?" Ginny asked, her arms crossed and a skeptical look on her face. "Slumming?"

"Visiting," said Jay. "Which reminds me, I should probably go check out the Junk Shop and let Dad know I'm here." He waved and quickly jogged away.

"Yeah, Evie and I are gonna head over to our side of the island," said Carlos, as they peeled away from the group.

"Going home too, are you, Mal?" asked Ginny. "What would your mom say, I wonder, if she could talk again? To see that her nasty little girl grew up to be so good?" She shook her head. “If you can change, I guess they’re right, there’s hope for all of us,” Ginny said in a soft, sweet voice, batting her eyelashes mockingly.

“Who’s they?” asked Mal, but Ginny, apparently bored with the conversation, was already walking away.

chapter 16

Gothic Style

Evil Queen had been exiled to the farthest, most remote, and practically abandoned part of the island, so by the time Evie and Carlos made it past Woeful Way and turned onto Hell Street, both of them were panting from the long walk. Without the fear of Maleficent, chaos had settled upon the Isle of the Lost and it appeared even the island's mostly undependable, rinky-dink transportation system had completely broken down. The goblins had abandoned their rickshaws, which were left to rust on the side of the roads.

Everywhere they went, they were met with frowns and scowls. Evie tried not to look too nervous for Carlos's sake, since he was obviously extremely uncomfortable with all the attention.

It didn't help that she was also exhausted and her feet hurt. Evie told herself exercise was good for the skin, and wiped her forehead with her handkerchief. She was still wearing her fancy dancing shoes with the high heels, and she almost fell in relief when they finally reached the familiar tall, gray stone walls of the Evil Queen's castle. Then she remembered she was afraid to face her mother.

She knocked on the heavy fortress door. "Mom?" she called nervously. "Um, it's me? Evie! Are you there?"

"It looks deserted," said Carlos, glancing askance at the cobwebs and dust.

"Oh, it always looks like this," Evie assured him. "Mom's big on personal maintenance, but housekeeping, not so much.

"Let me see if I can find the key," she said, walking over to the nearest wall and feeling for a brick that had come loose. "Here it is," she said, holding up an ancient rusted key. "Maybe she's out getting ready for the Anti-Heroes meeting?"

"Maybe. Wow, this place really looks like no one's lived here for centuries," said Carlos as they walked inside.

Evie bristled. "It's the height of Gothic style!"

"More like the bottom of it," said Carlos, scrunching his nose.

"Okay, fine, maybe it *is* a bit dark and dreary," said Evie, who had never been too bothered by the gargoyles and cobwebs until now. She looked around. Hmm. Maybe Carlos was right. It was a little dustier than she remembered. She took another step and sneezed.

"I'll wait here," said Carlos as Evie went off to check the bedrooms.

"Mom?" she called, gingerly stepping into the Evil Queen's room. Her mother kept it the way it had always been, when she had been queen of her kingdom and bent upon destroying Snow White. There was a dark silhouette in the middle of the room where the Magic Mirror used to hang before it had been broken into pieces, and a little podium in front of it where her mother would pose and preen, as if the mirror were still there to showcase her reflection.

The closet doors were open, blue gowns and black capes in disarray, white ruffs strewn over the floor. Her mother's traveling trunk was missing from the topmost shelf, and from the looks of the mess, Evil Queen had packed in a hurry. That was odd; where had she gone? Didn't she have to be back in time for the meeting tonight?

Evie noticed something else. In the center of her mother's dressing table was a large ebony box, one that Evie knew well. Her mother had schooled her in the art of beauty regimes from the pots and brushes, paints and blushes, eye makeup, foundation, and mascara in that very chest.

It was strange. Her mother had left behind her most

prized possession? Where could Evil Queen have gone without her makeup?

Evie walked down the grand staircase, still sneezing from the dust. She couldn't believe they had lived this way for so long, forgotten and unloved.

Carlos was nowhere to be found. Evie got a little worried and called his name, but there was no answer. Where was he? Evie didn't scare easily, and she was in the house she had grown up in, but it was strange to be here all alone, without her mom bustling around and pressuring her to try the latest exercise fad. She didn't even know where to start looking. The castle was so big that Evie never even knew how many rooms it had. She and Evil Queen had mostly stayed in the main area in the middle.

Maybe he was outside. She walked out the front door. "Carlos?" she yelled again.

"Over here!" he called. He was all the way on the other side of the castle, hidden by the overgrown weeds. In the moonlight, she could barely make out the tips of his black-and-white hair.

She walked over and found him standing in front of a series of stone steps that led to a cellar door. "Well, this is the place all right," he said, pointing to a sign that was hung on the front.

ALL ANTI-HEROES WELCOME,

MEETINGS ARE SATURDAYS NEAR MIDNIGHT

How strange, Evie thought, and for a moment wondered nervously if Evil Queen was just out at the market buying provisions for this very mysterious gathering.

"Is anyone inside? I don't even know where that door leads," she told him.

"No, I don't hear anything," he told her. "Any sign of your mom?"

"No." Evie told him what she found in the room. "It looks like she went away somewhere. She took her trunk, but left her makeup behind. But maybe she'll be back for the meeting?"

Carlos nodded. "Come on, let's go check out my place. Hopefully we'll be just as lucky there."

"But we didn't find my mom," said Evie.

"Exactly," said Carlos.

chapter 17

Terrible Two

Hell Hall was built in the style of an elegant Victorian mansion. Of course, since it had been transported to the Isle of the Lost, it was nothing but a rotting shell now. Carlos let them in through the side door. So far, everything was as he remembered. Cruella's mean-looking red sports car was parked in the garage, covered by a canvas sheet. The kitchen was still decorated in black and white tile, the refrigerator nearly empty. He peeked into the living room, and saw that it was exactly the same—the broken-down furniture covered with dusty white cloths, the standing knight's armor they kept in the hallway still rusty, the wallpaper still faded, and there were still holes in the plaster molding.

"Mom?" Carlos whispered.

Evie nudged him. "She's not going to hear you that way. Louder."

Carlos tried again. "Mom?" he croaked.

"CRUELLA? ARE YOU HERE?" Evie yelled.

Carlos almost fell to the floor in fright. "Don't DO that! Or at least warn me first!"

The kitchen was untidy, with dirty dishes in the sink and crusted food on the counter. Carlos began cleaning up almost automatically. It had been his job to keep house when he lived there. Cruella spent her days eating waxy old chocolate bonbons and watching the Dungeon Shopping Network.

"Doesn't look like anyone's been here in a while either," said Evie, sniffing. "I think I'm allergic to the Isle," she said apologetically.

"There's only one way to find out. Wait here," said Carlos. He steeled himself and went through the hidden passage to Cruella's treasured fur closet.

There was no way his mother would leave without her precious furs. They were all she cared about in life. He flung open the door and gasped. They were all still there—mink and ocelot, beaver and fox, rabbit and raccoon, sable and skunk. Alas, not one Dalmatian coat; Cruella's greatest regret. But he noticed that her rollers were missing from their case in her dressing room, along with the small overnight bag she often used when she went to visit the spa in Troll Town. (Apparently trolls were talented masseurs, due to their large hands.)

He walked back to the kitchen, where Evie was seated on a stool, blowing her nose. "She's gone?" she asked.

"Looks like it," he said, opening the cupboards for more clues. "And the milk in the fridge expired three months ago." He picked up the box and shook it so its contents sloshed. "Curdled."

"But the milk's always expired when we get it."

"Oh, right, I forgot," said Carlos, who wanted a huge delicious glass of fresh milk right now. Out of the corner of his eye, he saw a shadow move across the kitchen window and jumped. "Who's there!" he called.

No answer.

"I thought I saw something," he muttered, and not for the first time, he wished they were back home safe in Auradon. This wasn't home anymore, and it probably never had been, not really.

"She leave any clues?" Evie asked.

"No, just her furs," said Carlos.

"Interesting. But isn't Cruella obsessed with her fur coats?" asked Evie, who had once been stuck in that very closet, until Carlos rescued her from its bear traps.

"Obsessed is putting it mildly," said Carlos.

"Evil Queen left her makeup, and Cruella de Vil left her fur coats," said Evie. "But they're definitely both gone.

Maybe they thought they would be back quickly. I mean, they should be at the meeting tonight, right? Otherwise why would they leave the things that mattered to them the most?"

Carlos didn't point out how insane it was that cosmetics and furs were what mattered the most to their mothers. He was used to coming in second in Cruella's affections—make that third, after the car. Probably fourth, after the wigs, if he was being truly honest.

A twig snapped outside. This time Evie heard it too.

"Who's there?" Carlos called again, opening the door. "Show yourself!" he said, even though he was shaking in his boots. He wished Mal was with them. Everyone was scared of Mal.

He heard snickering in the bushes, and whispering. "It's him, it's really him. And her, I think that's her. The pretty one." Two figures stepped out to the light. One was tall and skinny and the other was short and round.

"Harry! Jace!" Carlos said.

"Your friends?" asked Evie.

"Not exactly," he told her. Harry and Jace were the sons of Cruella's most loyal minions, Jasper and Horace. The three of them used to hang out since their fathers were scared of Carlos's mother, and had forced their boys to befriend Carlos. They had helped decorate for the howler of a party Carlos had thrown for Mal at Hell Hall not too long ago.

"You're back!" said Harry.

"What are you doing here?" asked Jace.

"Can't a guy visit his mother?" asked Carlos. "What's up with you guys?"

"Nothing much. We saw you on the telly," said Harry. They sounded exactly like their fathers, down to their Cockney accents.

"At the Coronation?" Carlos said.

"Yar," said Jace. "When the dome broke and Maleficent zoomed out of here, fast as her dragon wings could take her, we all cheered."

"We thought it was finally our time, that she'd take Auradon for us!" said Harry.

"Evil rules!" cheered Jace, raising a fist.

"But o'course you all had to stand up against her, eh?" Harry shook his head. "And Mal, turning her mama into a lizard!"

"Mal's the new Big Bad, huh," said Jace. "She ever turn you into a lizard?"

"No," said Carlos.

"You scared of her?" Harry wanted to know.

"Of Mal? No," said Carlos again. "I used to be, but not anymore. Mal's . . . changed."

"Crikey! You mean she's a lizard too?" said Harry.

"No. Mal's not a lizard," he told them, rolling his eyes as Evie tried not to laugh. Carlos remembered why he didn't miss hanging out with Harry and Jace. Conversation tended to go around in circles. "Hey, do you guys know where my mother is?"

"Who?" asked Jace, affecting a blank look.

"Cruella de Vil!" yelled Carlos.

Harry and Jace exchanged shifty looks. "Don't worry 'bout your mama, now; we're here, right?" said Harry.

"Righto, guvnor, welcome home!" said Jace, with a menacing glint in his eye.

"Shhh," said Harry. "Don't spoil it."

"Spoil what?" Carlos wanted to know.

But the two junior henchmen wouldn't say and only laughed uproariously. Obviously, something was up, and it made Carlos's stomach churn. Harry and Jace had never been good at keeping evil schemes to themselves, and it sounded as if that's exactly what was about to hatch here.

chapter 18

Pirate's Booty

Jafar's Junk Shop looked as it always did, like a dilapidated dump. Through the grimy window, Jay could see the shelves filled with broken radios, lamps, and chairs as well all manner of old appliances that no one used anymore. Jafar had filled his mind with dreams of endless riches, and Jay used to imagine that all the twisted and rusted metal and the knockoff jewelry they sold would magically turn into piles of real gold and jewels. Of course, that never happened.

Jay picked the locks on the front door (all twenty-four of them) and let himself inside, skulking around a little, afraid of what his father would say when he saw him. "Dad?" he whispered. "Dad? Are you here?" he asked, a little more loudly. The air was musty and stale, and a fine layer of dust covered the gadgets and trinkets on the counters. There was no answer, until a rusty squawk from the back of the room echoed, "Dad? Dad? Dad?"

Jay ran to the private sitting area behind the shop, pushing back the heavy velvet curtains to find Iago, Jafar's loyal parrot, looking terribly scrawny and out of sorts, with molted feathers covering the newspaper at the bottom of his cage. The bird practically snorted and put his wings on his hips when he saw Jay, as if to say, *About time, kid!*

"Where's Jafar?" Jay asked.

"Gone," said Iago. "Gone gone gone gone gone."

If there was one thing Jafar could be said to care about, it was his loyal sidekick. Jay didn't think his father would leave Iago to starve, so wherever he'd gone, he must have expected to return shortly. Jay changed the newspapers and refilled the bird's water and cracker supply.

"You don't know where Dad went?" Jay asked.

"Gone gone gone gone gone" was all Iago said, stuffing his beak with crackers as fast as he could.

Jay sighed. The cranky parrot had never been much help in the past, so of course he was no help now. He checked the rest of the shop for any small clue or indication as to where Jafar could have gone, but didn't find anything helpful. Where had his father disappeared to? The only place the villains ever talked about going was Auradon; they were obsessed with returning to their true homes. Growing up, Jay recalled his father telling him how Agrabah was its most beautiful kingdom, with the Sultan's Palace and its golden domes high up north, past the Great Wall.

There was a knock on the door. "Are you open?"

"Sure," said Jay. "Come in!" He figured whoever it was might be able to tell him something about his father's disappearance.

Big Murph, a young pirate who ran with Hook's crew, walked in, an eye patch over one eye, a red bandanna tied around his forehead, and a faded yellow vest over a dirty T-shirt and holey shorts. Like the rest of his kin, Big Murph only wore shower sandals, even when it snowed. "Hey, Jafar, glad to see you open up again, we're out of fishing . . ."

The stout pirate stopped short when he saw Jay. "Oh! It's you!"

"Hey, Big Murph, what's up?" Jay asked. He liked Big Murph and the pirates. The big guy was usually friendly and Captain Hook had asked Jay to join their crew a couple of times, telling him they could use a talented thief among their ranks, but he had always passed. He wasn't a big fan of scurvy.

"JAY!" Big Murph said, looking fearful as a few more people wandered into the Junk Shop to browse. He looked around the shop. "You're really back?" he asked suspiciously.

"Yeah, I guess so."

Big Murph continued to look askance at Jay. "Is it

true—that Mal and Evie and Carlos are back from Auradon too?"

Jay leaned on a counter and crossed his arms, still unsure of what this was all about; the pirate was sure acting cagey. "Yes, we're here to, um, visit our aged relatives. Do you know where my dad is, by the way?" It was still hard to believe his father wasn't at home as Jay recalled that most days Jafar was too lazy to get up from his divan.

Big Murph shook his head and wouldn't meet his eyes.

"No clue, huh?" said Jay, who was starting to feel that the big man wasn't quite telling him the whole truth.

"Nope," said Big Murph stubbornly. "Shop's been closed and we've been out of fishing hooks." The pirates often fished from the piers.

Jay rummaged through the nearest drawers and found a bag full of hooks. "Here, take them," he told Big Murph.

"How much?" the pirate asked nervously as Jafar often charged ten times the amount the stuff was actually worth.

"Just take them," said Jay. It wasn't like he could spend those coins in Auradon anyway. His dad would scream at him for giving something away for free, but Jafar wasn't here right now, was he?

"Serious?" Big Murph asked skeptically.

"Yeah, go ahead, get out of here. Go fishing. Catch a crocodile while you're at it," he said with a grin.

A goblin brought up his items to the register and Jay rang him up. Big Murph was still standing there. "Guess it's true, then, what they say about you guys," the pirate said, almost defensively.

"Who's they and what do they say about us?" asked Jay, making change for the goblin.

But Big Murph wasn't paying attention anymore, as he was too excited about the bag of hooks. Then he checked the time on his pocket watch and jumped. "Oh, I'll be late! Gotta run! But maybe I'll see you later?" he said meaningfully.

Then he was gone before Jay could ask him any more questions. Was Big Murph talking about the Anti-Heroes meeting? He wasn't sure, and the bad feeling he had about attending this meeting only grew. Whatever it was, it had turned a happy-go-lucky little pirate into a shifty-eyed mercenary.

Before he could think on it too much, Anthony Tremaine popped his head in the shop as well. The handsome grandson of Lady Tremaine curled his lip when he saw Jay. "Oh, it's you," he said, sounding terrifically bored. He had the same haughty way of speaking as his grandmother. "I heard a nasty rumor that you and the other turncoats were back on the Isle."

"Turncoats!"

"Isn't that what you call someone who turns against everything they used to stand for?" asked Anthony. "That little performance at the Coronation was ever so . . . *good*, wasn't it?"

"What do you want, Anthony?" asked Jay, impatient to get rid of him.

"Jafar promised Mother a new shoe-stretcher," Anthony said. "I paid him but he hasn't delivered. I was hoping he was back to make good on our deal. Mother's beside herself." Anastasia still refused to wear shoes in the right size, preferring to buy them a size smaller so she could try to expand them through rigorous and hopeless toe-straining, as if Prince Charming would still change his mind.

"Hang on," said Jay, looking through the many shelves and drawers, but he couldn't find what he needed. "Sorry, looks we've run out."

"Even if the embargo's lifted?" asked Anthony with a smirk.

"Come again?"

"If you're back, it sure looks like Auradon's sending their trash to the Isle of the Lost again, doesn't it?" Anthony laughed, pleased with his insult.

"Ha-ha," said Jay.

"A joke," said Anthony, with a shrug. "What are you doing back anyway?"

"What's it to you?" asked Jay. "Who wants to know?"

"You know what, I'm too bored to pretend to care," said Anthony.

"Fine," said Jay, reaching out to shake Anthony's hand.

Anthony gave him a strange look, but shook hands with Jay before leaving the shop. Now it was Jay's turn to smirk, since he'd swiped Anthony's watch for old times' sake. It was so easy, just a flick of the wrist, flip of the latch, and it was his. Oh, he'd missed this. Jay counted the seconds for the snobby boy to return. One, two, three, four . . .

Anthony reappeared at the doorway, and he sure wasn't laughing now. "Give it back, Jay," he said fiercely. "Now!"

"What are you talking about?" asked Jay, the very picture of innocence even as his eyes twinkled with amusement.

"My watch. You took it."

"No, I didn't."

"Yes, you did!"

"I didn't take it, I swear. Maybe you just misplaced it," said Jay with a shrug. "You should be more careful with your things."

"It's a wristwatch! Where else would it be but on my wrist?" Anthony glowered and stomped off, muttering darkly to himself about how Auradon should keep its trash for itself.

Jay whistled as he closed up the shop again and waved goodbye to Iago, promising to send a goblin to feed him crackers. Anthony was right, Jay had stolen his watch, but instead of keeping it, he'd hidden it in Anthony's jacket pocket. He knew Anthony would go crazy looking for it, and would be especially annoyed when he discovered Jay "hadn't stolen it" after all.

Sometimes, even reformed villains needed to have a little fun.

chapter 19

The Mists of Auradon

While it had been hard saying goodbye to Mal and letting the four villain kids return to the Isle of the Lost, Ben knew that if anyone could get to the bottom of what was happening back there, she was the one to do it. He was glad she had her friends by her side as well. There was no point in wasting time biting his fingernails and watching the clock. He didn't realize he'd spoken out loud until Cogsworth interrupted his thoughts.

"Did you say clock, Sire?" his loyal servant asked. While Cogsworth was no longer a grandfather clock, he was still understandably sensitive when he heard anything pertaining to timepieces. "It is close to midnight, should you need the time." The stalwart Englishman was overseeing the footmen as they set down Ben's trunks from the journey in the royal bedroom.

"Thank you. I didn't realize how late it was. You can leave the rest for tomorrow," Ben said, dismissing them. He was incredibly tired, and the extra-plush mattress in his large wrought-iron four-poster bed was especially inviting after the lumpy one in Camelot. He was happy to be back in his room, with the familiar Auradon banners and exercise equipment, the huge yacht model he'd made still sitting on his desk.

"If I may . . ." said Cogsworth, pausing at the doorway. He waited for Ben to nod before continuing. "Lumiere mentioned you had encountered a rather purple dragon in the woods. Being that my old friend is prone to flights of fancy, I thought I would ask you myself. Is it true, Sire, about the dragon?"

"I'm afraid it is," said Ben. "May I ask that you and the rest of the palace staff please keep this news to yourselves for now? At the right time, I shall alert the general population of the danger."

"Of course, Sire," said Cogsworth, who had turned gray. "Do you think it is . . . *her*?" he asked, visibly shivering at the thought.

"Unfortunately, I can't think who or what else it could be but Maleficent," said Ben. "But don't worry, my friend, we'll keep Auradon safe."

Cogsworth bowed, and when he left the room, Ben noticed that everything had been unpacked and put away in pristine order even though he'd told him to wait until tomorrow. Ben had to smile. That Cogsworth: his loyal efficiency was regular as clockwork.

Even though he was exhausted, the events of the night meant Ben found it hard to fall asleep. Deciding it was useless to keep tossing and turning, he got up to do some work instead. When he turned on his computer, he found that as promised, Carlos had sent him the link to the Dark Net. Ben clicked around till he found the photos Mal had told him about on the Anti-Heroes thread. He was taken aback to find one of himself with a red *X* over his face too. He clucked his tongue and continued to read on, steeling himself for further assault and more invectives.

The Anti-Heroes forum was lit up that night, with many of its members posting their excitement about tonight's meeting. Then Ben saw a new post that caught his eye. The message read, *Looks like four former castoffs have washed ashore on the Isle of the Lost. Prepare Operation Welcome Home!*

Hang on.

Four former castoffs?

That could only mean his four friends, right? Ben checked the time stamp. The message was sent an hour ago, about the same time Mal and the gang would have arrived on the island. He had to warn them that their presence had been noticed by their enemies. Ben sent texts and tried to call, then remembered that the island was cut off from the main servers. If Mal got into trouble, there was no way for him to find out until it was too late. He could send his royal troops after them right now, but since nothing had happened yet, he knew Mal would take it as an insult. Ben slammed down his laptop, frustrated.

He would just have to trust that she, Evie, Jay, and Carlos would be able to deal even if the situation got out of hand. He forced himself to stop worrying and focus on the current problem instead—the purple dragon of Camelot. Earlier, he had sent emergency e-mails to his council, alerting them to the danger he'd discovered. Grumpy and the dwarfs advised they were up for battle, axes at the ready, although perhaps the best thing to do would be to destroy Maleficent while she was in her tiny lizard form in her glass dome. Others were more cautious in their response, however.

An e-mail had arrived from the three good fairies. Merryweather, the youngest, and most capable with modern technology, had sent their reply.

Our dearest king,

It is with great concern that we received the distressing news about Camelot's dragon. While it does seem as if none other than our old nemesis Maleficent is behind such mischief, we would like to advise caution in this arena before we jump to conclusions.

If the creature is indeed a shapeshifting evil fairy, it is best to obtain proof before we act accordingly. Perhaps it would be possible to retrieve an item linked to the dragon in question? A nail from its claw? A piece of its hide? A lock of its hair?

If you are able to recover such an item, it would be prudent to bring it to Neverland right away, the ancestral home of the fairies, so they can ascertain the identity of this dragon.

Without proof that it is indeed Maleficent, it seems imprudent to act with violence toward the lizard in the library, who might still be innocent.

Your godparents,
Flora, Fauna & Merryweather

He was glad they agreed that Maleficent should not be harmed, as he knew he could never face Mal if she returned on Monday to the news that her mother had been destroyed without a fair trial or even proof that she was the one rampaging through Camelot.

The royal technicians had set up several cameras all around Maleficent's prison, and Ben called up the screens. All of them showed a tiny lizard under glass, and so far there was no indication it was anything other than that. He closed the windows showing the security screens with a sigh.

As he was typing a grateful reply to the good fairies, there was a knock on his door. "Enter," he called.

"Forgive me, Sire, but Archimedes just dropped this off. From the way he was hooting, it seemed rather urgent," said a sleepy Lumiere, handing him a letter that had beak marks around its edges.

Ben ripped open the letter, his heart pounding as he imagined what news Merlin had sent from Camelot. Had the dragon scorched the castle? Laid waste to the entire kingdom?

All well here. Purple dragon spotted off Charmington Cove, thought you should know. It appears the creature is on the move.

Not the greatest news, knowing the dragon was venturing into other areas of Auradon, but at least, not the worst news either.

Lumiere was standing at attention, awaiting orders. "It looks like we'll have to pack up again," Ben said. "But I'll drive this time."

"Very good, Sire," said Lumiere.

"Oh, and find Chad Charming; tell him to be ready to leave with me in the morning." It would be best to have someone who knew the lay of the land. No matter that his and Chad's friendship had cooled slightly since the villain kids had enrolled at Auradon Prep.

Ben turned back to his computer, and reread the good fairies' words. If the purple dragon was in Charmington, he would make sure to bring a piece of it to Neverland so they could solve the mystery of the creature's identity once and for all.

chapter 20

Bargain Bin

If it could be said that the Isle of the Lost had a jewel in its crown, then Maleficent's former home, the Bargain Castle, would be it. The old place didn't look half as good these days, however, with its peeling paint, bolted doors, and shuttered windows. Mal wasn't sure what she thought she would find in there, but after using a stick to pry off the panels that had nailed the door shut, discovering that the whole place was completely ransacked was a surprise. When Maleficent ruled the island, her boar-like henchmen at her command, and goblins to do her bidding, no one would even dream of knocking on their door before a decent hour. But now . . .

Mal picked her way through the destruction. The slimy contents of their fridge were spilled on the floor, and her mother's former throne looked as if it had been raided for its upholstery, with bits and pieces of foam and feathers sticking out of the huge holes that had been ripped and torn or clawed from its seat.

The queen was dead (well, she was a lizard). But there wasn't a new queen either. The Isle had fallen further into chaos and disrepair. While its citizens feared Maleficent, she had brought a semblance of order to their hardscrabble lives, and now that she was gone, it was total anarchy.

Mal made her way to her room, wondering what she would find, and a bit anxious about the small but real treasures she had kept there. When her mother had shipped her off to Auradon, there was no expectation that she would actually stay there, and so Mal had left most of her things back home. She opened the door, expecting to see it similarly looted and plundered.

But her room was just like she had left it. Purple velvet curtains, bureau with all her little sparkly doodads, her many sketchbooks and canvases stacked neatly on the bookshelves. "Huh," she said. Why was her stuff left untouched?

Mal grabbed a backpack from her closet and began stuffing it with the things she wanted to bring back to Auradon: her journals and sketchbooks, a necklace with a dragon-claw charm that her mother had given her on her sixteenth birthday (in fact, it was the first—and only—gift she'd ever received from Maleficent that she'd felt like keeping). When Mal was eight her mother had gifted her with an apple core; at ten, with fingernail shavings. Maleficent explained they were part of spells, but since there was no magic on the island, it just seemed like an excuse to give her daughter trash.

"Hello?" a voice called from the main room, and Mal heard the sound of footsteps coming closer. "Is anyone in here?"

"Who is it?" Mal asked, stepping out of her room warily.

"Mal! You're really back!" The girl who stood in the middle of the living room was tall and rangy, wearing black from head to toe, with a tight jacket and leather pants.

"Mad Maddy?" Mal said, excited to see an old friend. When they were little Mad Maddy and Mal were practically twins since they had the same color hair. But when they got older Maddy liked to change it to a different shade every week. Right now it was bright aqua green to match her eyes.

"It's just Maddy now," she said, with a witchy giggle. "But just as mad as ever. I saw that the door was open and I thought it might be you. Everyone's saying you guys are back; news travels fast on the Isle."

"I bet," said Mal. "Do you know who did this?" she asked, motioning to the gutted living room.

Maddy took a look around. "Goblins mostly, but almost everyone came here after the Coronation. I saw Ginny

Gothel wearing one of your mother's capes the other day."

"Ugh!" said Mal. Ginny really was more rotten than she had remembered. "Well, at least no one touched my room; isn't that odd?"

Maddy took a seat on the broken sofa, which looked as if it had been used as a trampoline for a school of goblins, and put her booted feet up on the smashed coffee table. "Of course not, why would they?"

"What do you mean?"

Her old friend pulled at her green hair, twirling it around her finger. "We all saw what you did, after all."

"What I did?"

"To your mother. You turned her into a lizard. You beat Maleficent," said Maddy, as if the words were more than obvious.

"Is that what everyone thinks around here? That I *wanted* that to happen?" asked Mal. She'd only wanted Maleficent to stop attacking her friends, to leave the good people of Auradon alone, and she'd had no idea that by doing so her mother would be greatly reduced in size and power.

"Well, didn't you?" said Maddy, sorting through the rubble to see if she could scavenge anything worthwhile. "It's what happened, isn't it? We all saw it."

So that was why her room had remained untouched. The Isle no longer feared Maleficent. Now they bowed to a new ruler. They feared Mal.

"It's not what you think," said Mal.

"Doesn't matter," said Maddy with a shrug. "It's what everyone thinks."

"Well, they're wrong." Mal kicked an overturned chair.

Maddy startled. "Wait, what? You mean it really wasn't you? You didn't do it?"

"No, I mean, I guess I did, but it was her fault she had so little love in her heart, which is why she turned into a lizard," explained Mal, blushing to use the word *love* in front of Maddy. They'd both grown up thinking love was for fools, morons, and imbeciles, after all.

"Hmm," said Maddy, studying Mal closely.

"What?" asked Mal.

"Nothing," said Maddy. "Come on, let's go get something to eat."

chapter 21

Frenemies

They still had ample time before the meeting, so when Carlos mentioned that he was hungry, Evie suggested they walk back into town to the Slop Shop to get something to eat. After refusing to tell them any more about what they knew about Cruella's whereabouts, Harry and Jace had run off, giggling mysteriously to themselves, and she was glad to be rid of their company.

"You think they were telling us the truth? That they don't know where my mother is?" asked Carlos.

"Who knows, between those two I'll be surprised if they remember their names," said Evie, once again cursing herself for forgetting to change into comfortable footwear.

"Where do you think they are, then?" asked Carlos, playing with the zipper on his jacket. "Our parents, I mean."

"My guess is they'll be at the meeting later," said Evie. "Don't you think?"

"What are we going to do when they tell us what their evil plan is?" said Carlos. "I'm not sure I can stand up to Cruella the same way Mal stood up to Maleficent, you know?"

"We'll figure it out when it comes down to that," said Evie. "Don't worry, I'm not looking forward to seeing my mother either. I know she'll hate the way I'm doing my hair now."

When they reached the goblin-run café, they noticed Mal in the window, laughing with a girl Evie didn't recognize. The two of them were giggling together while sharing one of the Slop specials—stale bread pudding topped with rancid banana syrup, a popular dessert on the Isle of the Lost, where extracts from rotten fruit were their only source of sugar.

"Who's that girl?" Evie asked.

"Oh, that's Mad Maddy," said Carlos. "She and Mal used to be tight."

"I don't remember her from Dragon Hall," said Evie.

"Yeah, she transferred to an all-witches school on the other side of the island in ninth grade," said Carlos.

"Witches. Even if you can't practice magic on the island, they still think they should teach their kids about it."

He led them to the counter and ordered snacks. The goblin grunted and shoved two steaming-hot cakes on paper plates their way.

"Ah," said Carlos, making a face as he bit into a hard, sour scone. "Just like I remembered." He spit it out. "Although I think I'll pass. I don't think I can eat this anymore."

Evie nodded, and put hers back on its plate, untouched.

"Oh, hey, guys, come and join us," Mal called from her table.

Evie took a seat next to Mal while Carlos pulled up a chair next to Maddy. Mal was digging into her pudding. "Want some?"

Carlos nodded. He found a clean spoon and took a bite. "I forgot how much I used to like these things," he said, and took another heaping spoonful.

"You did?" Evie blanched.

"You didn't?" said Maddy, looking her over with a sardonic smile. "Wasn't this an intrinsic part of your childhood?"

Evie returned the girl's up-and-down gaze. "Not mine," she said coolly. "My mother and I hardly came into town. Actually, make that never."

"Sorry, don't you guys know each other?" Mal asked, to make up for the awkward silence that ensued. "Maddy, this is my friend Evie, and Evie, this is Maddy. We grew up together."

"Yeah, Carlos told me," Evie said.

"We liked to hex our dolls together," said Maddy. She smiled sweetly at Carlos. "Hey, Mal, remember when we covered Hell Hall in fake spiders?" she asked. "Or were they real?"

"They were real and real dead," said Mal, laughing at the memory. "It took forever to collect so many!"

Carlos squirmed in his seat. "Yeah, that was fun, not really," he muttered.

"Carlos screamed so loud when he saw them, I thought he would wake up Cruella," Maddy cackled, and put up her hand for a high five, which Mal slapped with gusto.

Mal and Maddy were still laughing over their past exploits, which Evie found highly annoying. They hadn't returned to the island to gossip with old prank-mates. Plus, they shouldn't be making fun of Carlos. Evie realized she wasn't looking at Auradon Mal. This was Dragon-Hall Mal, the sneering, scary girl who used to stomp through the island with a scowl and a can of spray paint. Evie cleared her throat to get their attention. "So, Maddy, do you guys have any idea where my mom is? Or Carlos's? We just went home and they were nowhere to be found."

Maddy crumpled her napkin and pushed her bowl away just as a goblin came by and grumpily reminded them that there was no lingering at the tables.

"You really don't know?" she asked coyly.

"No, we really don't," said Evie, who had had it with this girl's snickering innuendo. Maddy was acting as if she knew a wicked secret and wouldn't share.

"Do *you* know anything?" Mal asked Maddy.

Maddy shrugged. "No one knows anything about anything." She continued to eat her pudding, a sly smile on her face.

Evie didn't like the girl, but even if she did, she knew Maddy was lying. She knew something about where Evil Queen, Jafar, and Cruella de Vil had gone, that was for sure. Was she in cahoots with them and this Anti-Heroes club? Evie wouldn't put it past her.

It was almost time to head over to the Anti-Heroes meeting, and Evie felt herself break out in a cold sweat, imagining what was in store for them. Evil Schemes was only a class taught at Dragon Hall, but Cruella de Vil, Evil Queen, and Jafar could spin an evil scheme in their sleep. They lived and breathed for malice and revenge. Who knew what kind of terrible surprise their parents had cooked up for their return?

chapter 22

Needle in a Haystack

Chad Charming wasn't particularly happy to have been woken up at dawn on a Sunday, and was still complaining about it as Ben drove them down the Auradon Coast Highway that morning in the royal convertible. The handsome prince groused that he had been up late from Castlecoming festivities the night before, and what was so important that they had to leave this early?

"Really, old man, why on earth are we going to Charmington? Mom's going to freak when we get there; you know she likes to have everything sparkling clean for a royal visit," said Chad.

"I told you, I have an early meeting with the grand duke

about the upcoming ball," said Ben, who wasn't about to tell Chad about the dragon menace just yet. "And you know the fastest way to get there."

"Fine," said Chad, leaning back in the passenger seat. "Keep on this lane and then exit at Belle's Harbor, then we can take the back roads until you get to the Stately Chateau."

Ben did as directed, glad that Charmington Cove wasn't stuck in the past like Camelot, and he could actually drive his own car without the burden of the full royal entourage. If he could have taken his motorbike, he would have, but the sporty coupe was fun to drive too. Plus, he'd been meaning to talk to Chad about something.

"Hey, Chad," he said. "What's up between you and Jay lately? Have you been giving him a hard time?"

Chad snorted. "Those villain kids are getting big heads, don't you think? Strutting around Auradon like they own it. Someone's got to put them in their place."

"Their place is in Auradon now," said Ben angrily. "Look, man, they're just trying to fit in. Give it a rest, will you?"

Chad squirmed in his seat but he nodded and said he would.

Ben relaxed his hold on the steering wheel, satisfied. As pompous a prince as Chad was, he wasn't a complete jester.

They arrived at Charming Castle by noon. Chad hollered for his parents, but was told they were out running errands for the upcoming ball and wouldn't be back till late.

While Chad went up to his room to get some more sleep, Ben met with the grand duke, who was in charge while the royals were away. The duke was polishing his monocle in his receiving room when Ben was announced. He bowed to Ben and offered him a seat on one of the tufted red velvet chairs across the large inlaid table.

"You got my message last night?" Ben asked. "I'm sorry for the rush."

"Oh yes, Sire," said the grand duke, his mustache quivering. "As you requested, I sent messengers throughout our kingdom to see if anyone else had encountered such a creature. My men are very thorough, and they understand this is just as high a priority as Operation Glass Slipper. According to your note, we are looking for any sign of a purple dragon, am I correct?" He cupped his mouth and whispered, "Like Maleficent?"

"Unconfirmed for now," said Ben. "As far as we know, she remains safely locked away in the library."

The grand duke looked relieved. "When she was turned into a lizard, she did seem quite harmless—cute even, if I can say so, Sire. I hear lizards make good pets."

Ben was noncommittal and the grand duke remembered the pressing business he had to communicate to Ben. He pulled up a few scrolls. "I received this just before you arrived. Other than the report that Merlin received of a creature spotted off Charmington Cove, it appears there hasn't been any fire damage or livestock stolen, nothing of that sort. However, there was another incident this morning down by Cinderellasburg."

"What kind of incident?"

"A creature was spotted in a chicken coop early this morning," said the grand duke. "However, the farmer reports that the animal did not resemble a dragon. More like a purple snake."

Snake. Dragon. Lizard. It was all part of the reptilian family, Ben thought. "It could still be related to what I'm looking for; let's check it out."

Ben left Chad back at the castle, snoring away, and the grand duke and a team of his footmen accompanied him to the pretty little village that Cinderella had once called home. The farmer and his wife were expecting them, standing nervously in front of their homestead. They bowed and curtsied when they saw Ben.

"I understand you saw a strange-looking snake on your farm this morning?" he asked.

"Yes, Sire, it came out of nowhere and took three eggs from the coop!" the farmer's wife told them. "Largest snake I've ever seen, for sure, and very purple. I screamed my head off."

"Great fangs too," said the farmer, shivering. "We're lucky it didn't take a sheep . . . or a cow."

"Would it be possible to see the coop?" Ben asked.

"Of course, Sire," the farmer said. "This way." The

couple led them around the house to where a tidy-looking chicken coop stood in the middle of their backyard. Several fat fluffy chickens were pecking seeds on the ground.

The farmer opened the door to the coop and Ben knelt down to look inside. It smelled like straw and feathers, and something not entirely pleasant.

"What are you looking for?" the grand duke asked, lifting his monocle. "I can send the footmen to search."

"No need," said Ben as he had spotted something glittering in the nearest nest. He picked it up with his fingertips, careful not to crush it since it was very delicate. "I think I've found what I was looking for."

"What is it?" asked the grand duke.

Ben stood up and held it up to the light. It was a glittering scale. Purple. The exact shade of the dragon he had seen in Camelot. He put it carefully in his handkerchief and slid it into his pocket.

"Thank you, you've been very helpful," he told the couple. "My staff will send you a dozen eggs for your trouble."

"Thank you kindly, Sire," said the farmer, tipping his hat.

"Yes, very good, very good indeed, thank you for your quick response," said the grand duke. "And do let us know if you see it again."

Ben turned to leave, but the farmer's wife stopped him. "Please, Sire, there's a rumor going around that Maleficent isn't as securely imprisoned as we think. That she's been attacking Auradon again. Might she have something to do with the snake I saw today?"

"Where did you hear that?" he asked, worried.

"My cousin lives in Camelot Heights, said there's a purple dragon over in their parts causing havoc and making a mess of everything."

"Ah."

"Is it Maleficent?"

In answer, Ben pulled up his phone and showed her the feed from the dozens of security cameras installed around the room that showed the tiny lizard napping on a rock. "What do you think?"

The farmer's wife didn't look convinced. "She could be getting out and then coming back in. Crafty, she is."

Ben had to agree with that. "Let us know if you see the snake again, but please try not to worry. I've sent several troops of imperial soldiers to Charmington to keep it safe."

Ben returned to the castle to pick up Chad and took his leave of the grand duke, who promised to alert him should anything else purple turn up in the area. Chad was in the kitchen petting a brown puppy from Bruno's latest litter.

"All set, old man?" he asked.

Ben nodded. "Let's go. I'll drop you off back at school on my way."

"Where are you going?" Chad asked as he climbed back

into the convertible. "Maybe I'll join you. I've got nothing better to do today but homework. Now that Evie won't do mine anymore."

"Neverland."

Chad changed his tune. "Right. I'll stay at Auradon Prep, if you don't mind. One of the Lost Boys is still mad that that I stole his bear costume last time they played us. He brought it up again at the game yesterday, but it wasn't my fault he never got it back!" The ragtag group was still very fond of their bear, fox, rabbit, and raccoon pelts.

"But it was *your* fault that someone found it and turned it into a rug," reminded Ben.

Chad sighed. "Yeah, you might have a point there."

chapter 23

Down the Rabbit Hole

Jay was hiding by the hedges that lined the road to Evil Queen's castle when he heard the voices of his friends whispering—or was that bickering?—in the darkness. "Hey," he said, stepping out from behind the bushes. "About time you guys got here." It was 11:54, only five minutes before the meeting.

"I broke a heel," said Evie, who was limping a little. "Sorry. I'm still wearing dance slippers, not hiking boots. I forgot how much walking we have to do on the island. But I'm okay."

"What were you guys arguing about?" he asked.

"Evie doesn't trust Maddy," said Mal, and filled him in

on what they'd learned so far from their brief time on the island, mostly nothing good. Evil Queen, Cruella de Vil, and Jafar were still nowhere to be found.

"Mad Maddy? I wouldn't trust her either; she's pretty shady," said Jay. "This is the Isle of the Lost, remember? Isle of the Lost, Land of Lies."

"Find anything at the Junk Shop?"

"Not a thing," said Jay, who told them about how suspicious and odd Big Murph had acted, and how Anthony Tremaine had called them turncoats.

"They all hate us," said Evie, who sounded sad about that fact.

"Yep, we're totally despised," agreed Carlos.

"They don't *all* hate us. Some of them are really scared of me, it turns out," said Mal.

"Everyone was always scared of you, Mal. That hasn't changed; come on," argued Carlos.

"Okay, fine," admitted Mal. "But now they're even more scared!" She told them about how her room had been left pristine while the rest of the castle was ransacked. "Apparently it's because they all think I'll turn them into lizards."

Jay guffawed. "You *should* turn the Isle of the Lost into the Isle of the Lizards!"

"Not funny," said Mal, even though her lips were quirking a little. "And we still have to find out what this Anti-Heroes club is planning."

"Planning their revenge on us, most likely," said Carlos.

"Do we have to go to this meeting?" asked Evie.

"Come on, let's not chicken out now. Maybe they just don't like sandwiches? Heroes? Get it?" joked Jay.

The rest of them groaned. Mal ignored his wisecracks. "Well, from how Maddy was acting, it sounds like Jafar, Cruella, and Evil Queen are definitely part of it."

"Looked to me like Maddy is part of it too," said Evie.

"Oh, definitely," said Carlos.

"Shhhh!" warned Jay. "Someone's coming."

The four of them melted back into the shadows, peeking out from the hedges to watch as a succession of shadowy figures made their way toward the cellar door. "Recognize anybody?" whispered Evie.

"No," said Jay, who had the sharpest eyesight. "It's too far and too dark to see."

"What do we do now?" asked Carlos, trying to push the branches aside so they didn't tickle his nose.

"We follow them in, isn't that obvious?" Mal said, mimicking the tone he'd used on them earlier.

"No bickering!" said Evie. "And quiet, or they'll hear us!"

A few more dark silhouettes made their way down the road toward the castle, disappearing down the stone steps. After a large wave of people, the crowd trickled down to a few stragglers. "Okay, let's go," said Jay. "We'll sneak in after those guys." He scanned the area. "I think they're the last ones."

The four of them crept up from behind, and when the

clouds drifted from the moon, they saw that the guys they were following were Harry and Jace. Carlos shrugged his shoulders when his friends turned to him questioningly. Although Jay thought that if the sons of Cruella's most loyal minions were part of this club, then it probably meant Cruella was one of its leaders.

Harry and Jace disappeared down through the cellar door, which was left open. They waited for a beat then followed right behind. The castle dungeons were cold and damp, and as they made their way deeper and deeper into the darkness, through winding corridors and musty hallways, it grew colder and darker still.

Jay was in the lead, and when he suddenly stopped short, the rest of the group piled behind him, stumbling and pushing into each other. "Oof!" "Ouch!" "Watch it!"

"Where'd they go?" Carlos whispered. "Why'd you stop?"

"I think they heard us," Jay whispered back. "Everyone, be quiet!" He strained to hear and squinted in the pitch-black gloom. A few moments later, he picked up the sound of Harry's heavier footsteps. "All right, come on," he whispered, motioning to his friends to follow him.

"Where are they going?" Mal asked Evie. "This is your castle, right? What's down here?"

"No idea," said Evie. "Until today I didn't even know we had a basement."

The darkness abated somewhat and they saw Harry and

Jace disappear into a room on the left side of the hallway. Jay nodded and the four of them entered right after. Like the rest of the dungeon, the room was completely dark, but Jay thought he could sense people around them. What was going on? He couldn't help but feel that their sneaky entrance hadn't been so successful after all.

"Back up, back up, I have a bad feeling about this," he said, trying to lead them the opposite way.

Too late!

The door immediately shut with a bang behind them.

"Dalmatians," cursed Carlos. "It's a trap!" It was just as they feared, the stuff of their nightmares.

From the darkness came a menacing voice. "Operation Welcome Home is a go."

chapter 24

Warm Welcome?

Carlos startled at the sound of the voice and quickly hid behind Mal. He figured it was the safest spot. He wasn't afraid to face danger, but he preferred to do it knowing Mal was in front of him. Evie gasped but managed not to scream. Jay cracked his knuckles, preparing to throw fists. Mal was calm, and her voice was even and steady when she poked Carlos and told him what to do. "Torch, please."

"Pardon?" he asked, before realizing she meant the torchfire zapp on his phone. He turned it on, shining a blazing light into the darkness.

The four of them were illuminated by the sudden brilliance, and Carlos saw that they were surrounded on all sides by a small but excitable group of young villains. He recognized some of the faces—his cousin Diego de Vil, who raised an eyebrow in greeting; Harry and Jace with eager grins on their faces; Yzla, Hadie, Claudine Frollo, Mad Maddy, who was holding some kind of flaming weapon in her hands.

Hold on. What was that noise? What were they doing?

He couldn't be sure at first, but it looked as if the crowd was clapping, cheering even, hooting and stomping feet and calling out their names. "They're here! They're here!" "It's really Mal!" "Jay's here too!" "Yay, Carlos!" "Evie looks fantastic!"

And hang on . . . that weapon that Maddy was holding . . . was that a cake? With way too many candles?

It was definitely a cake, and one that said WELCOME BACK, HEROES!

"I think they mean us?" said Jay, breaking into a grin.

"Definitely us," said Evie, sounding incredibly relieved.

"Hmm, I think we had the wrong idea about this club somehow," said Mal, nudging Carlos. "Or maybe we're at the wrong meeting? They sure don't seem very anti-hero to me."

But Carlos didn't notice the ribbing, he was too stunned to see a very familiar and very welcome face in the group.

"Professor!" he called, when he spotted none other than his former Magic of Science teacher, Yen Sid. He was standing right behind Maddy, the stars on his peaked sorcerer's hat reflecting the candle flames. Yen Sid was one of Dragon Hall's most respected teachers, even if it was rumored he wasn't any kind of villain at all, but had voluntarily relocated to the Isle of the Lost in order to help educate the villains' children.

"My boy," said Yen Sid with a grave nod. "Welcome." He turned to the gathered group. "Give them space, give them space, don't crowd them around so much," he said gruffly. "And I suggest you four deal with those candles before they set fire to the whole building. We wouldn't want Evil Queen returning home to a pile of ashes, now, would we."

The four of them blew out the cake to another round of cheers. Someone turned on the lights, and Carlos realized they were in a perfectly normal-looking basement room, clean and bright. There was a chalkboard on one wall and rows of neatly arranged tables.

"Shall we begin with the cake? I had to bribe some hard-bargaining mice to sneak it out of the Auradon kitchens to the goblins earlier this week just for this," said Yen Sid. "Yzla, bring over the plates, please. Maddy, will you do the honors?"

"Of course, Professor," said the young witch, and set about cutting slices.

The four of them watched in stunned silence as the group obediently and graciously moved aside and sat patiently, waiting for their slices. Carlos caught Jay's eye and shrugged.

Yen Sid motioned for them to take the nearest table. "At least they're not here to attack us," said Jay, who accepted his slice with a wink.

"Unless they want to kill us with sugar," said Mal, looking forlornly at her piece. "I sure wish I hadn't eaten that whole stale pudding now."

The Anti-Heroes club members, who'd never had anything remotely this good, were gobbling up the cake as fast as Maddy could slice it. It was their first taste of real sugar, and a few of them were dizzy and ecstatic from the sweetness.

Harry and Jace walked up with triumphant smiles on their faces. "Told ye we wouldn't spoil it, and we didn't, did we?" said Jace. "Ye had no idea, right?" asked Harry eagerly as he licked some frosting from his upper lip.

"No idea," said Carlos, suddenly feeling much fonder of them than before. They were slow and bumbling, but often eager to please. When he had been forced to throw that party for Mal, they had helped him decorate without complaint. Jace and Harry grinned and shuffled back to their seats, satisfied.

"Professor, can we ask what this meeting is about?" said Evie as she picked daintily at her slice of cake.

"In time, in time," replied the professor, licking frosting off his mustache. "We have much to discuss, and it is better to do so on a full stomach." He set his plate down on their table. "So tell me, how were you able to return to the island?"

"I drove," said Carlos, his mouth full of cake.

"We stole the royal limousine," said Jay. "It has the clicker that unlocks the dome and makes the bridge appear."

"Clever," said Yen Sid. "I'm sure your talents at thievery were helpful in that area."

Jay beamed. "I guess so."

"Although we ran into Prince Ben and he let us take the car anyway," reminded Mal, rolling her eyes at Jay for taking all the credit.

"Yes, Ben was always a progressive thinker," agreed Yen Sid. "And you are all well, I take it? Enjoying life on Auradon?"

"Yes, sir," said Evie. "Very much so."

The professor stroked his long gray beard. "Excellent, excellent. Do give Fairy Godmother my regards when you see her next."

Evie promised to do so. "By the way, Professor, does my mother know you're here in our basement? Is she part of this?"

Yen Sid chuckled. "Everything will be explained in time."

Mal was fidgeting and looked impatient, and Carlos knew she was eager to put an end to this chitchat, but Yen Sid seemed determined to keep the conversation light.

"How are the Knights doing this season?" he asked the boys.

"So far we're five and one," said Jay. "We've won all our games except a loss to a strong team from the Imperial Academy. Li Shang doesn't mess around."

"In my day, the Olympus team was the force to be reckoned with—always difficult to beat the gods," Yen Sid said, looking nostalgic at the memory.

"They still have a strong lineup, but a lot of the god kids enroll at Auradon Prep now, so maybe that's why," said Jay.

Carlos finished his cake and was bursting with curiosity. He couldn't keep it inside anymore. "So, Professor, come on, tell us, what is this whole Anti-Heroes thing all about?"

"I can certainly explain," Yen Sid exclaimed jovially. "After all, I founded it."

chapter 25

One More Fairy Tale

In the past, the only way to get to Neverland was to fly. Just like the Isle of the Lost, there had been no usable bridge connecting the tiny island to the mainland, so the fairy court used to leave a bottle of fairy dust at the dock. Then visitors would sprinkle it on themselves while thinking happy thoughts, lifting into the air and floating to Neverland. When Ben was little, he had loved to travel by fairy dust, but when King Beast and Fairy Godmother decided that even this magic was against Auradon policy, a proper bridge was built.

Even so, Ben couldn't help feeling a bit disappointed that he wouldn't be flying anywhere that day.

He dropped Chad off at school and was in Neverland by midafternoon, driving across the bridge and onto the winding, curvy roads of the hilly island. He thought he was following the map correctly, but it looked like he'd taken a wrong turn somewhere, and instead of arriving at the fairy homestead, he found himself parked next to a group of tepees.

Ben left the car to ask for directions. There weren't that many other people around, and Tiger Peony, Tiger Lily's daughter, was the first person he encountered.

"Hey, Ben," she said, when she saw him. "Come to gloat?"

"Excuse me?" he asked, before realizing she meant the tourney game that Neverland's team had lost the day before. "Yeah, sorry about that. Lost Boys played hard."

"Everyone's bummed," she said. "Mom's already sworn to train a bunch of new recruits. What are you doing here?"

"I'm headed to Fairy Vale," Ben said, "and I got lost. Can you show me the right way?"

"Sure," she said. "Are you here about the dragon?"

Ben stopped. "How do you know?"

"Everyone knows. It's Maleficent, isn't it?"

"Actually we don't know for sure," he said. "That's why I'm here."

Tiger Peony seemed to think that was a reasonable answer, and didn't ask anything more. She pointed back down to the forest. "You just make a left at the waterfall instead of a right, and the road should take you straight to the Great Oak in the vale. They'll be waiting for you."

The fairies lived in a thousand-year-old oak tree that was as large and roomy inside as any royal palace in the kingdom. They flitted about, their wings buzzing, excited to greet Ben, their laughter like the sound of tiny little bells ringing. Faylinn Chime, a tiny fairy who had golden hair and translucent wings, greeted Ben with a smile.

"What can we do for you, Ben?" she asked.

"The three good fairies sent me. They said you might be able to help me with a problem we're having," he said, taking a seat at a large oak table that was carved right from the tree.

"We heard about Camelot's dragon," she said, her voice grave. "Is the creature still at large?"

Ben nodded. "And if I'm right, it was just in Charmington this morning." He removed his handkerchief and showed them the purple scale from the chicken coop. "Do you know what this could be from?" He handed it over as gently as possible.

Faylinn picked up the scale and showed it to the other fairies. "Looks like a serpent of some sort," she said.

He held her gaze. "I need to know if it's from Maleficent."

She considered his request. "We can check the archives. We fairies have cataloged every kind of creature across every kingdom in Auradon, so if it's from Maleficent, we'll be able to tell you for sure," she said, putting the scale back in the handkerchief and motioning to the fairy next to her. "Take this to Lexi Rose, and have her run a few tests to see if it matches anything we have in our database."

"Thank you," said Ben.

"I'm glad you're here," said Faylinn, "because we were just discussing whether to come to you with what we've found."

"Oh, what's up?"

"Ben, I don't know if the three good fairies or Merlin have told you, but here in Neverland, we fairies are very sensitive to fluctuations in the atmosphere and the world around us. I've heard that in Auradon, you have been experiencing a series of earthquakes, is that right?"

"Yes, and aftershocks too."

"We've been having terrible weather, storms from the coast out of season, as well as giant waves crashing on our shores."

"Yes, all around Auradon, the weather's been acting strangely. I just heard it snowed in Northern Wei, and hailed in Goodly Point," he said. "Scientists hope it just means winter's coming early."

"We don't know what's really behind it yet, but I've sent letters to all the great minds of Auradon, telling them our concerns. And according to our fairy calculations, whatever this is, it started in the Isle of the Lost," said Faylinn.

"I've already sent a team over to investigate there," Ben

said, thinking of Mal, Evie, Jay, and Carlos. "I have confidence they'll get to the bottom of whatever is happening there."

"Glad to hear that," said Faylinn. "Why don't you wait here; it shouldn't take too long to discover the origins of that scale you found. We'll get you something to eat and drink. You must be tired from driving around all day."

"Thanks, Fay."

He stood and she bowed to him. She began to fly away then called over her shoulder, "By the way, when you get home, please tell Chad Charming we hope he's enjoying his bear rug." She winked. "And if he ever pulls something like that again, I'll fetch Captain Hook from the Isle of the Lost to teach him a lesson."

"Will do," Ben promised.

chapter 26

Anti-What?

When she had been a student at Dragon Hall, Mal had never been lucky enough to take one of Yen Sid's classes, and so while she knew about his mysteriously "good" reputation, she wasn't as prepared as the others for his lighthearted demeanor. "First of all, how did you know we would be here?" she asked.

"Well, once you received our messages, of course we began to prepare for your arrival," said Yen Sid.

"That was you!" exclaimed Carlos.

"Of course it was. We couldn't sign them without giving ourselves away—too many bad eggs around, you know, one can never be too careful—but we hoped you would figure it out, and you did," said the professor. "I'm very proud of you."

"But how were you able to reach us?" asked Jay.

"Freddie!" said Mal. "She was the messenger, wasn't she? Because she just transferred over from the island, and so she knew how to use the Dark Net, and how best to get in touch with us."

"You are correct," said Yen Sid.

"What do you mean?" asked Carlos.

"I saw her at the library one night, I had a feeling she was following me. Plus, she's the only villain kid in Auradon who didn't get a message to return home," Mal explained. "And she must have known I'd only take it seriously if it sounded as if mine was from my mother, which is why she wrote 'M.'"

"But you still haven't told us what this group is all about?" asked Evie.

The old sorcerer removed his hat and scratched his bald pate. "Before I explain further, let's clean up," he said. "The club knows there are different rules here, about keeping things orderly and neat. Slovenliness is a hard habit to break, but they're trying."

"Here, let me," said Mal, gathering the plates while Evie grabbed the cups and the boys wiped their table down with napkins.

Mal tossed the plates into the trash, and looked up to

see a group of younger kids staring at her with a worshipful look on their faces.

"What you did in Auradon, we think it was awesome," Hadie, Hades's blue-haired son, whispered.

"It really was," agreed Big Murph.

"So cool," piped in Eddie, with a snaggletoothed smile just like the one his father used when he was intent on drowning Duchess and her kittens.

Soon an admiring crowd had gathered around her, and Mal noticed similar groups were forming around Evie, Carlos, and Jay as well. "You guys really think so?" she asked them. "That what we did at the Coronation was awesome?"

"Of course!" Hermie Bing squealed, sounding just like an elephant in her father's old circus.

For a moment, Mal believed they were all excited and impressed because she was the baddest in the land, but it soon became clear that it was just the opposite. All they wanted to talk about was how good she'd become. Mal couldn't get over how wrong she and the other villain kids had been about the club.

"Wait a minute—I thought everyone was scared of me because you guys think I'm worse than my mother," she said, holding up her hands.

"Oh, we *are* scared," said Harry. "Totally scared to find out that the power of good is stronger than the power of evil!"

"Wait, so you guys aren't angry at me? You don't hate us?" she said, though she felt kind of silly even asking at this point, considering the cake and everything else.

The babble of excited voices rose in indignation. "No!" "Not at all!" "We love you guys!" "What is she talking about?" "She's been gone, remember? She doesn't know things have changed."

"We want to *be* you, we want to learn how to do what you did," said Big Murph earnestly. "We want to learn how to be good too."

"See, when we saw what the four of you accomplished, we realized that we don't have to do what our parents want us to do either," said Hadie. "Though, admittedly, it might be a little harder for me, considering. But I want to be different."

"We choose to be good," said Yzla forcefully, as if this statement was a rebellious act somehow, which, considering they were in the Isle of the Lost, it truly was.

They explained that the club was formed right after Mal defeated Maleficent. The island's misfits, many of whom had already failed Lady Tremaine's Evil Schemes class and sometimes surreptitiously helped hobbled goblins cross the street rather than kicking them to the curb, realized that they were drawn to goodness rather than evil.

In a way, Carlos had been right, the Anti-Heroes movement *was* a radical group, especially since it was devoted to unraveling every tenet of the island's dearly held wicked values. Mal's actions on Auradon had sparked a revolution, one in which the new generation of villains on the Isle of the Lost were eager to follow in her footsteps. Mal had expected to find a group devoted to hating heroes, not to be the center of hero worship. It took a while to believe that they were sincere, but eventually Mal was convinced.

Of course, the members of the club told Mal and her friends they had to practice this new inclination in secret, which is why even the villains who were at the meeting had been rude to Mal and her friends out in public. No one could know that the members of the club were trying to be good, especially not on the Isle of the Lost. But thanks to Yen Sid, they had a place to be themselves now. Yzla explained that Yen Sid suggested the Castle Across the Way because it was far from town and had been deserted for a while. Plus, no one would suspect that anything but the plotting of evil schemes or cosmetics lessons was under way in the home of Evil Queen.

"Wait! So she's definitely not here? Evil Queen isn't part of this group? What about Cruella or Jafar?" Mal asked.

Before anyone could answer her question, Yen Sid stepped up to the blackboard. "Welcome to the weekly meeting of the Anti-Heroes," he said. "We are now formally in session."

"Can I ask why you're called Anti-Heroes?" asked Carlos, raising his hand.

"Don't you know? Think about it," said the professor, his eyes twinkling.

Mal scrunched her forehead, and reflected on what she had just learned from the excited group of so-called villains. "It's called Anti-Heroes because you're hiding in plain sight," she said.

Yen Sid smiled broadly. "It is the only way to hide."

To anyone who stumbled on the Anti-Heroes thread on the Dark Net, it looked as if the club despised the foursome, but of course the photos of the four of them were simply recruitment tools, subtly telling members-in-the-know that this was the place to be if they wanted to be like Mal, Evie, Jay, and Carlos. Mal shared her epiphany with the group, and heads happily nodded around the class.

"That is part of it, of course, but there is another reason we are called Anti-Heroes," said Yen Sid. "What most people don't know is that *anti-hero* is another word for villain—or let me put it this way, an anti-hero is the villain that you root for in the story. An anti-hero is a hero who isn't perfect. An anti-hero doesn't ride up in a white horse, or have shining golden hair and wonderful manners. In fact, an anti-hero doesn't look like the typical hero of a story at all. Anti-heroes can be crude and ugly and selfish, but they are heroes nonetheless. As flawed as an anti-hero is, they're still trying to do the right thing. You are all anti-heroes, and I'm proud of you." He beamed at them, and the group clapped and cheered.

"So just to confirm, this is a secret club to teach villains—sorry, *anti-heroes*—how to be good?" asked Carlos. Mal remembered how Ginny Gothel had said "they" were right about Mal, and "there was no hope for anyone"—she must have meant there was little hope for evil anymore, if even Maleficent's daughter had chosen to be good.

Mal frowned. "Hold on, Professor. If this club is devoted to learning how to be good, am I right in assuming Evil Queen, Cruella de Vil, and Jafar have nothing to do with it either?"

"With the Anti-Heroes? No, of course not, they're villains through and through, I'm afraid," said the professor. "But speaking of the villains, it is very fortunate you understood our message to return to the island, as we desperately need your help in locating and outwitting them."

chapter 27

Anti-Heroes' Secret

"Wait! So they're not here? They're really gone?" asked Carlos. "My mother, Evil Queen, and Jafar?" He tried to temper his relief at the news. As much as he had convinced himself he was ready to stand up to his mother like Mal had done to hers, he was more than happy for the respite.

"And if you guys don't know where they are, does that mean they're not on the Isle of the Lost?" asked Mal.

"Not exactly on the island, no. But not exactly off it either, at least, we hope not," said Yen Sid, remaining maddeningly obscure on the subject. "Let me backtrack a little. It appears they vanished from the Isle of the Lost soon after

Maleficent broke the dome open, but no one knows for sure. People panicked when they saw Maleficent turned into a lizard; they feared that Auradon would seek revenge on the island. In the chaos and breakdown that ensued, it was hard to notice anything out of the ordinary since everything was out of the ordinary, especially with the goblin embargo.

"No one thought it strange that Jafar didn't open up shop for a while, as he was often irregular in his habits, and Evil Queen and Cruella de Vil mostly keep to themselves. But then the Junk Shop remained closed, and a few weeks later, a goblin who delivered the daily basket of supplies to Evil Queen's castle reported that no one ever took them inside. They were just piling up by the front door, and even Cruella's wigmaker remarked that she hadn't come in for her regular fitting, so we knew something was wrong." He frowned and tugged his beard. "I sent messengers to each of their homes, and runners across the island to see if anyone had seen them anywhere, but to no avail. They were well and truly gone."

The rest of the group nodded, and it was clear this was old news to them. Carlos noticed that some of them were doodling in their notebooks or passing notes and whispering. Even if they were trying to be good, they were still naughty kids. He tried to ignore them and focus on what Yen Sid was saying.

"But if they're not on the Isle, where could they be?" asked Carlos with a gulp. "You don't think they're in Auradon, do you?"

Yen Sid gazed balefully at his young pupil. "Before I answer your question, I would like to ask a few questions of my own."

"Shoot," said Mal.

"Have you been experiencing a series of earthquakes in the mainland? Small tremors, vibrations? And once in a while, a real rumble?" he asked.

"Yeah, we have," said Jay as the four of them nodded in agreement.

"Have you noticed if they are becoming stronger and more frequent?"

"They certainly are," said Mal. "I know Ben's council is worried about it, since it's never really happened before. Not just earthquakes, though—he mentioned that the whole kingdom is suffering from unseasonal weather: frost, hurricanes, sandstorms."

"Then it is as I suspected," said Yen Sid. He sighed.

"What does the weather have to do with the missing villains?" asked Mal.

But the professor was already scribbling in his notebook and ignored her question. When he looked back up at them, he had their full attention. "I think it's time for me to tell you a little about the history of the island. As you know, when the villains were placed on the Isle of the Lost, Fairy Godmother, under King Beast's command, created the invisible dome to keep magic out of their hands so that they would never threaten Auradon's peace again."

"I thought it was also because they were being punished for their evil deeds," said Evie.

"In effect, it was a punishment, as they were kept here mostly to ensure the safety of the kingdom," said Yen Sid. "But what we didn't realize then was that keeping magic off the surface of the island created tremendous pressure in the atmosphere, and the magic that was kept out had to go somewhere else."

"Energy transference," said Evie knowingly, even as the rest of the club was falling asleep on their stools. It was obvious they'd all heard this before.

"Yes," said Yen Sid, impressed. "I warned Fairy Godmother about the risks of the establishing the magical barrier, but at the time, we deemed it a better gamble than letting the villains run amok in the country with their magical powers intact."

"Magic was pushed underground," said Mal slowly.

"Exactly. Over the course of the twenty years since the dome was created, magic grew wild and flourished underground, where it created a system of tunnels, the Endless Catacombs of Doom, which compose a series of magical lands underneath ours," said the professor. He looked at them somberly. "Some say these tunnels also include an escape route out of the Isle of the Lost and straight into Auradon itself."

"Auradon!" cried Carlos.

"Yes, and this passage must be closed before anyone

discovers it. I fear we might already be too late," the professor said.

"A magical underground land right beneath ours that leads to Auradon," mused Jay. "Wild."

The professor frowned. "I sent a letter to King Beast explaining my conclusions, but I suspect Evil Queen, Jafar, and Cruella de Vil intercepted it. Maleficent's goons used to go through my mail, and I'm certain that Evil Queen did the same thing when Maleficent was gone."

"Ben is king now, by the way; maybe you should have written to him," Mal chided. "What about the tremors—the earthquakes, the weird weather we're having—are they related to this, then?"

The professor nodded. "When Maleficent broke open the dome when she escaped, I believe that the magic that was released sparked something underneath the Isle of the Lost, which caused a ripple effect in the weather that can be felt all the way to Auradon, and has caused unusual natural phenomena."

"Sparked something?" said Mal. "Like what?"

The professor was about to answer when Carlos changed the subject back to his pressing worry. "Excuse me, Professor, but they must have found out about the secret tunnel. The escape route," he said. "Cruella, Evil Queen, and Jafar, I mean."

"So that's why they packed light," said Evie. "They thought they'd be in Auradon soon, where Cruella could buy new furs and my mother could get her hands on this season's cosmetics, and Jafar probably thought he could fetch Iago back as soon as they took over Auradon."

"But if they're in Auradon, someone would have reported them by now," said Jay. "I can't exactly see them blending in with the locals."

"No, I don't believe they are in Auradon," said Yen Sid. "They were headed there most likely, but no, they are not there yet."

"But you said they're not in the Isle of the Lost either," said Carlos.

He startled when Evie suddenly straightened in her chair. "The Magic Mirror!" she cried. "That's why the mirror couldn't find them! Mal, remember how we were wondering if they were using some kind of powerful magic to hide themselves? And we were right—sort of—there was powerful magic, but not the way we thought."

Yen Sid looked pleased. "Were you ever in my class?" he asked. "You have an extraordinary talent for logic."

Evie flushed happily at the compliment. "Thanks, Professor."

Jay looked around the table. "So where are they exactly? I don't follow."

"They're lost in the Catacombs," said Mal crisply. "They were trying to get to Auradon, but they got lost somewhere along the way."

The old wizard nodded. "Almost. They are not lost. It

is my belief they are down there searching for something."

"Something other than the way out?" asked Jay. "What could be down there that they want?"

Yen Sid motioned to the group to close their books and put their maps away. He sighed heavily and looked each of them in the eye. "Where do you think evil comes from?" he asked.

"The Isle of the Lost?" offered Carlos.

"Close." His voice thundered in the small room. "Evil is a real thing, it lives and breathes, it works its malice through living vessels eager to spread its vile wickedness, but villains cannot be villains without the source of their power."

The younger members of the club began to whimper.

"Every villain has a talisman. These talismans hold the powers that were stripped from them upon their exile to the Isle of the Lost."

"Like the Dragon's Eye scepter," said Mal. "That was my mother's talisman. Are you saying there are other talismans in the Catacombs?"

"You would have been a good student in my class as well," said Yen Sid proudly. "Yes, the Catacombs of Doom are only one part of the equation. Like I said earlier, when Maleficent escaped, she released so much energy into the surrounding area that it sparked a magical reaction underground and caused the recent earthquakes and unseasonal weather phenomena all over Auradon. I'm afraid she's also awakened four evil talismans that have been growing in the Catacombs of Doom over the years. These talismans are growing in power, and causing havoc with our weather as they draw energy to themselves. Four of these talismans are the most dangerous right now: the Fruit of Venom, the Golden Cobra, the Ring of Envy, and a new Dragon's Egg."

An audible silence filled the room, and it was apparent that while the club knew about the Catacombs, learning of these talismans was new to the villains on the Isle of the Lost as well as the four visitors from Auradon.

"A *new* Dragon's Egg?" asked Carlos. "What does that mean?"

"Hang on," said Jay. "Does this have anything to do with the Dragon's Eye staff back in Auradon? The original?"

"Yeah, that one broke when Mom turned into a lizard," said Mal. "We found it and Ben put it away in the museum. It's useless now, so I guess this would be its replacement."

Yen Sid nodded to show she was correct. "Merlin wrote me about Camelot's problem, and along with the strange weather patterns worsening in Auradon, I realized I had to get you kids back to the island right away. There isn't much time, we must act, and quickly," said the professor. "The talismans desire to be found; they have already seduced their masters into looking for them and soon they will call others to their side. They seek to escape the darkness of the underground so they can once again bring chaos and catastrophe to our world above. You must find and disarm them before they fall into the wrong hands, then bring them back to Auradon, where they can be destroyed forever."

"We'll go as soon as we can," promised Mal.

"Remember how the four of you were able to defeat Maleficent?" Yen Sid asked.

They nodded.

"But what if it wasn't just Maleficent and the Dragon's Eye you were facing? What if you were facing all four villains holding their talismans? Imagine facing not just Maleficent and her scepter, but Jafar and his Golden Cobra, Evil Queen and her poisoned apple, and Cruella de Vil and her Ring of Envy?"

"Oh," said Carlos. "That does not sound good."

"Used together, these four talismans for evil can overcome the power of good once and for all."

chapter 28

The Sorcerer's Apprentices

This was so much worse than she thought. Evie knew that this trip to the Isle of the Lost would mean they would discover that the villains were plotting yet another scheme, but she hadn't been prepared to hear about this. To think that there were four evil talismans out there, and that if their parents got ahold of them, they would be unstoppable was too frightening to contemplate. Since Mal had defeated Maleficent, Evie felt assured that they could handle whatever happened next, and that the power of good would always prevail. But now it sounded as if they were truly in peril once more.

Thankfully Mal still appeared calm as ever. "At least

now we know that's where they are, underground, in the Catacombs, looking for the power that they lost."

"Yes," said Yen Sid. "The four of you must find these talismans and destroy them before your parents can use them against Auradon. I'm afraid you're the only ones who will be able to outsmart them. After all, no one knows them better than you. Mal, even if Maleficent is in no shape to retrieve the Dragon's Egg, it's still imperative that you recover it before anyone else does."

"Great, let's go," said Jay, already up from his seat.

"First we must show you what we are working on." Yen Sid nodded to the assembled group, who sat at attention now, pulling out detailed maps and charts. "We think we are close to getting an accurate map of the underground tunnels."

"You've been in the tunnels, then?" asked Carlos.

"No. None of us have."

"But then how can you draw maps of somewhere you've never been?" said Carlos, confused.

"With the help of a little research," Yen Sid told them. He nodded to the class and they raised the books they were reading. "We stole them from the Athenaeum of Evil, of course." *A Brief History of Evil Talismans. The Legend of the Golden Cobra. Poison Fruit from the Toxic Tree. The Dragon's Eye Scepter: Lore and Myth.* "According to the books, each talisman is grown by magic in its ideal habitat, and so we have been sketching their possible landscapes," he said, as if it were as simple as learning how to plot an evil scheme, or how to trick a mark out of its money, when it was probably as difficult as teaching a jolly crew of pirates table manners.

"Great, you guys have maps to share. All right, then; just point us to the Catacombs, and we'll be on our way," said Jay.

"Well, that's where I'll need everyone's help tonight. We haven't been able to discover the exact location of the entrance to the Catacombs," said the professor. "We don't have much time left, so you and the rest of the Anti-Heroes will need to scour the island until you find it."

He began to give the members their assignments, sending them to every part of the island, from Henchman's Knob to the Blown Bridge.

"Shall we go with them?" asked Jay as the Anti-Heroes started to trickle out to search.

"Yes, but please remain where you are for now. Before I send you four off on this journey, I have a few words of advice to give each one of you. Acquiring these talismans will be very dangerous. Evil is seductive; you will have to remain strong and not fall prey to its temptations."

He stood in front of Carlos first and placed a hand on his head. "Carlos de Vil, you possess a keen intellect; however, do not let your head rule your heart. Learn to see what is truly in front of you."

Evie was next, and Yen Sid did the same, resting a hand above her dark blue locks. "Evie, remember that when you believe you are alone in the world, you are far from friendless."

Jay bowed down and removed his beanie so the good professor could lay his hand on his head too. "Jay of Agrabah, a boy of many talents, open your eyes and discover that the riches of the world are all around you."

At last he came to Mal. Yen Sid delicately touched her purple head. "Mal, daughter of Maleficent, you are from the blood of the dragon and carry its strength and fire. However, this burden is not yours to bear alone. Rely on your friends, and let their strength carry yours as well."

Yen Sid surveyed the young villains in front of him. "What you are about to do is very dangerous."

Carlos perked up. "That's fine, my middle name is—"

"Oscar," said Evie. "We know."

The group of Anti-Heroes burst into applause as Mal, Evie, Jay, and Carlos shook hands with the professor and thanked him for his wisdom and guidance.

"We will collect the maps that we do have," said Yen Sid. "Give us a few moments." The group began to disperse to begin their respective assignments, talking excitedly among themselves.

Carlos said goodbye to Harry and Jace, who had been tasked with searching near the Bargain Castle. Jay promised the pirates he would send them postcards from Auradon.

Evie was glad they had figured out where their parents

were, but going after them wasn't going to be easy. If Evil Queen was set on getting back her talisman of power, there was no stopping her. The woman elbowed people out of the way for a tube of concealer.

"Heading out to search?" asked Harry.

"Uh-huh," said Evie.

"Glad you guys are the ones going after them and not me and Jace. We'd be too scared, all right. Crikey, you're all so brave."

"I'm not, really," said Evie. "But sometimes you have to do the things you have to do. Thanks, though." Before setting off, however, she had to make sure she could move properly. She inspected her broken heel. She couldn't keep going this way; the Endless Catacombs of Doom sure sounded like they would entail a lot of walking as well, and she was still wearing the wrong shoes.

"Professor," she said, holding up her broken heel. "Do you think you can fix this with a little magic of science or something?"

He examined her shoe. "No, I'm afraid there is no way this can be salvaged through the magic of science."

Evie's face fell as she resigned herself to stumbling her way through the underground, her feet blistered and callused.

"But I do have something that might help you," said Yen Sid.

"What?"

"Tape," he said as he deftly taped the broken heel back to its original shape.

It wasn't a pair of sneakers, but at least she wouldn't be limping anymore.

While Yen Sid went back to going over the possible locations for the entrance to the Catacombs with Jay and Carlos, and the rest of the club members waited patiently for their assignments, Evie looked around the crowded room and didn't see Mal anywhere. Where had she gone? Evie took another look and caught a glimpse of bright aqua-colored hair swishing in the dark hallway, with Mal's purple head following behind.

At first she thought that maybe Maddy just wanted to talk to Mal privately, but when the two of them didn't return after a few minutes, she had a darker feeling about it. She peeked into the corridor and saw Maddy heading out of the basement and up the cellar stairs, with Mal following behind. Where were they going?

Already wary of Maddy's friendship with Mal, Evie decided to follow them to see what they were up to. She looked behind her to make sure the boys were still talking to Yen Sid. She wasn't spying on Mal; she was just being careful, she told herself. Mal had to have a good reason for going off with Maddy, didn't she?

Maddy was out of the basement now and heading down

the path away from the castle. Mal was following behind at some distance. They weren't walking together, Evie realized now. Mal was following Maddy, for some reason. But why? Who cared about Maddy?

They had to go find the entrance to the Catacombs; there was no time for this. Cruella de Vil, Evil Queen, and Jafar had a head start on them. If any one of them was able to lay their hands on their talisman, no one in Auradon would be safe. The foursome had to get going. What was Mal doing?

Evie lagged behind, trying to put some space between them, when Maddy stopped suddenly and looked around. Mal ducked behind a tree and Evie quickly hid in the shadows as well. She wasn't sure what was going on, but she was glad she hadn't let her friend go off alone like this.

The two girls kept walking farther and farther away. Evie followed behind.

chapter 29

Double Trouble

When Maddy left the meeting, Mal's first thought was that her friend wanted to get a head start on walking to Troll Town, where her group was going to search. Mal wanted to take a break too, before the four of them had to embark on this journey even deeper underground. The aqua-haired girl ascended the stone steps, and Mal was about to call out to her when Maddy checked her watch, picked up the speed, and disappeared into the maze of streets.

Mal also couldn't help but notice that Maddy kept looking over her shoulder nervously as she made her way through the dark alleyways. When she took off through the back way, cutting across Hell Hall's garden, going right instead of heading left for Troll Town, it became clear that she wasn't going where she'd been assigned after all. Mal watched as she ducked behind a corner, and overheard bits of a whispered conversation between Maddy and an unknown stranger. Something about "Catacombs" and "Doom Cove."

What was going on? Why wasn't Maddy going with her group? And who had she been talking to?

Mal's curiosity was piqued and she decided to keep following her. The group could figure out the plan with Yen Sid, but she wanted to find out what her old friend was up to.

She followed Maddy through the maze of streets, down Pain Lane and past Goblin Wharf, which was desolate and abandoned instead of the usual hive of goblin activity. Mal wished she could send her friends a text explaining where she was. She just hoped they wouldn't worry; she'd be back as soon as she found out what Maddy was doing.

Maddy led her back on the main road, and Mal had to lag behind farther so she wouldn't be caught. They passed the Bargain Castle and Maddy kept going, headed down Bitter Boulevard and right to the end of the island by the Rickety Bridge.

Maddy stepped onto the bridge and whirled around. "Mal, you can come out now, I know you're following me."

"You got me," said Mal, stepping into the light and walking toward Maddy. She knew when the game was up.

"Why'd you leave the meeting so fast? Is something going on?"

Maddy peered around in the dark. As far as Mal could see, there was nothing. The waters were black, and there was no one else on the bridge. Just the sound of the waves and the light from the Shattered Lighthouse. "Yes," said Maddy hesitantly, as if unsure whether to trust Mal.

"What?" asked Mal.

"Before the meeting, I got an anonymous letter saying that Evil Queen, Cruella, and Jafar would be returning from the Catacombs after midnight. They would be at Doom Cove."

"But why didn't you say anything at the meeting? Why go alone, then?" asked Mal, not sure if she believed her. She'd always had fun with Mad Maddy, but Evie was right, there was something off about her. Why hadn't she seen it before? Maybe because she was having too much fun indulging in old, bad habits?

Maddy's green eyes blazed. "Don't you see? The Anti-Heroes are the only ones who even know about the Catacombs of Doom! Yen Sid warned us that there might be double operatives in the club. I couldn't take the risk of letting them know that I knew."

"But who could it be? Everyone seemed so sincere," said Mal, wondering who had betrayed them.

"It could be anyone. They're a bunch of villains, Mal, come on. Do you really believe all of them would give up just like that? The professor thinks everyone is redeemable, but that can't be true," sniffed Maddy. "Of course there's a bad egg in the bunch. I can always smell one."

"Who do you think it is?" asked Mal.

"My money's on Harry or Jace—their fathers are still Cruella's loyal minions."

Mal considered this. It was hard to believe that anyone back at the meeting could be so two-faced, and Harry and Jace seemed more bumbling than malicious. "Maybe someone else on the Isle knows that Cruella, Jafar, and Evil Queen went down into the Catacombs to look for the talismans. It doesn't have to be someone in our group. If the three of them knew about it, they might have told someone before they left."

"Maybe," said Maddy. "But I doubt it."

"Who were you talking to back there?" asked Mal.

"Oh, just some goblin. I told them to find me if they catch sight of Jafar, Cruella de Vil, or Evil Queen."

"Show me the message," said Mal.

Maddy handed her the note, written in green ink. *Doom Cove. Prepare for our return to the Isle of the Lost. Talismans acquired. Alert the troops.*

"That's Doom Cove right there," said Maddy, pointing to the dark, sandy stretch of beach below.

"Who are the troops?" wondered Mal. "You don't think they mean a goblin army, do you?" There weren't enough villains on the Isle to put together a real battalion, and "troops" signified that whoever had sent the message was readying for a large-scale operation.

"Of course it means a goblin army, how else would they take down Auradon?" said Maddy.

"Are you sure you didn't tell anyone about it?" Mal asked, thinking of the conversation she'd overhead earlier.

"Duh, like I told you, of course not. No one can know!" said Maddy.

"We need to get help. I'll go back," said Mal, turning away. Maddy was obviously lying about telling someone, and Mal figured the easiest way to handle it was to get backup.

"No! We need to stay here, in case they do arrive. What if we miss it and they slip away?" said Maddy. "We should follow them and call for help later so we don't lose them. Don't you trust me?"

Mal understood that Maddy was testing her, and while she had a feeling that she shouldn't stay, she realized it wasn't safe to leave Maddy on her own at this point. She had to figure out what the girl was up to.

chapter 30

Seeds of Temptation

Carlos and Jay were so absorbed in their conversation with Yen Sid that they didn't notice that half of their team had absconded. The professor handed them the maps to the underground land. "These contain all we know about the Catacombs as well as the talismans. I hope you find them useful on your journey once we find the entrance," he said.

They thanked him, but Carlos was intent on learning as much as he could about the talismans before setting off underground. "So can we touch them? The talismans, I mean?" he asked the professor. "Or are they cursed? Like the Dragon's Eye?"

"Yeah, I don't look forward to falling asleep for a thousand years," said Jay.

"I'm not certain. My hunch is that each of you should be immune to your particular talisman, as Mal was unaffected by the curse of the Dragon's Eye."

"Anything else you can tell me about this Golden Cobra?" asked Jay.

"It should be an exact replica of your father's cobra staff. It's said that the Golden Cobras give up their freedom when they succumb to their master's power, but they are very much alive. It is a living weapon."

"Great," said Jay. Under his breath, he told Carlos, "I'm sure it'll just lie down and roll over for me."

"It's a snake, Jay, not a dog," said Carlos. "You should know the difference." He turned to Yen Sid, who was erasing lines on the blackboard. "About this Ring of Envy, what exactly does it do?"

"Your mother made everyone believe their lives were nothing compared to hers. That huge green ring that she wore was a testament to her glamour, and its size and great worth always made others feel small and useless."

Carlos swallowed a gulp, especially since his mother had always made him feel small and useless even without the aid of a talisman. "What about the Fruit of Venom; is it filled with poison?"

"Poisonous thoughts," said Yen Sid. "Taking a bite of it will fill one's mind with your deepest fears and insecurities, every kind of dark, malevolent emotion and idea, and the power to use them against other people."

"Yikes," Carlos said. Evie was one of the sweetest girls he knew, and he hoped she wouldn't be swayed by such a toxic influence. "And the Dragon's Egg?"

"The most powerful talisman of all, of course, with the ability to command all the forces of evil to do its mistress's bidding. Power is its own most powerful enticement. Moreover, Mal has wielded the Dragon's Eye staff, so she has already experienced the depth of its capability for universal dominance. She must be particularly wary of succumbing to its siren song."

"You hear that, Mal?" Carlos said, turning around, expecting to see Mal and Evie at their seats. But there was no one there. "Hey, where'd they go?" he asked Jay. "Mal and Evie—they're gone."

"That's weird, they were just here," Jay said.

"Yeah, well, they're not here now," said Carlos, annoyed. Most of the members had already headed out on their assignments, but Carlos ran around the room asking the remaining few if they had seen Mal and Evie.

"Yo, they bounced out with Mad Maddy," said Yzla. "But I don't know where they went."

"Mad Maddy? Why would they leave with her?"

Yzla shook her head. "Aren't Maddy and Mal friends?"

"Yes, but . . ." said Carlos, seriously agitated by now. Why had the girls taken off without telling him and Jay? It wasn't like Mal or Evie to just disappear like that. He was about to freak out when Evie burst back into the room.

"Guys!" she called.

"Where have you been!" Carlos demanded. "And where's Mal?"

Evie caught her breath. She'd been running and her cheeks were flushed. "If you stop yelling at me, I can tell you."

"Sorry," he said quickly. "We were just worried."

"Carlos was worried," said Jay. "I knew you guys would be back."

"Mal went off with Maddy. I think they're headed toward Doom Cove. I don't know what's going on, but I have a bad feeling about this," said Evie. "I heard Maddy say something about the Catacombs, so I thought I'd come back and grab you guys in case something happens."

"Let's go," said Carlos. "Doom Cove is a hike."

chapter 31

The Rescuers

Jay knew all the shortcuts through town, or at least he thought he did. Thinking it was faster to stay off the little alleyways, he led them up to Mean Street instead, but soon realized his mistake. They were farther from Doom Cove than if they had just taken Pain Lane down to Goblin Wharf as Evie had suggested. "Sorry, I thought this would be faster," he huffed, removing his beanie and wiping his forehead with it.

"It's okay, let's just get there," said Evie as they ran down the cobblestone streets, their heels kicking up dust as they garnered curious looks from a few townspeople. "Hurry!"

At last they made it past the Bargain Castle and had a clear shot all the way to Rickety Bridge. "Wait!" said Evie. "We don't want to give ourselves away."

"But where are they?" asked Carlos, scanning the bridge. "I don't see them."

"I distinctly heard Maddy say they were going to wait right here; maybe whatever they're waiting for has already happened?" Evie said, with a sinking feeling in her chest. "I should have stayed here! Curse these shoes, they slowed me down too much."

Jay focused on the bridge. It looked deserted and lonely in the moonlight, but at the very edge of it, he spotted two brightly colored heads—one blue-green and one violet. "There! I see them!"

Evie swirled to where he was pointing. "Let's move closer," she said, and they inched their way to the edge of the shore, as close to the bridge as they dared without giving away their presence.

"What are they doing?" asked Carlos. "They're just looking out into the water. What are they waiting for?"

"A goblin barge maybe?" guessed Evie. "Don't they work the graveyard shift?"

Jay scratched his forehead under his beanie. "Explain to me again why we're sneaking around? Why don't we just tell Mal we're here?"

"No!" said Evie. "Not just yet."

"Why not?" asked Carlos, who looked like he thought Evie was being a little paranoid.

"Because I don't trust Maddy, and if we tell them we're here, we'll never find out what she's up to," she told them.

"You just don't like witches," said Jay.

"No way!" said Evie, annoyed that she wasn't being taken seriously. "You guys seem to have forgotten I'm a witch too! Just like my mom. And I like myself just fine."

"You're a witch?" Carlos said. "Oh, right, you *are* a witch. I did forget."

Evie nodded. "It's okay, people tend to forget. Everyone just thinks I'm an evil princess."

They watched Maddy and Mal looking intently at the dark water, and after a few minutes, the boys started to get bored. "Come on, Evie, let's just tell Mal we're here. We need to start looking for the entrance to the Catacombs," Jay said.

"Just a little longer," Evie begged.

"I just don't see what the point of this is," said Jay. The two of them were still arguing over it when Carlos nudged both of them in a panic.

"What?" said Jay, annoyed.

Carlos couldn't speak, he just pointed—and they all turned their attention back down to the Rickety Bridge, where a group of villain kids had emerged from the shadows and quickly surrounded Mal and Maddy. It was a motley group, including Anthony Tremaine, Ginny Gothel, and the burly twin brothers Gaston and Gaston.

"Evie was right, this doesn't look good," Carlos whispered.

"Shhh!" said Jay, listening intently to the group's conversation.

Anthony Tremaine's rich baritone boomed through the air. "Look what we have here, the little heroine of the story," he said.

"What story would that be?" said Mal.

"Oh, just a little fairy tale they're spinning in Auradon about how wonderful it is that villains can change." He smirked. "What a shame we don't believe in fairy tales here."

"That's not true, there are people right on the Isle of the Lost that believe it too," said Mal. "Maddy, what's going on? Why are they here?" she demanded.

"Tell her, Maddy," cackled Ginny Gothel. "Tell her why you brought her here."

Back where they were hiding, Carlos stood on his tiptoes since the large silhouettes of the Gastons blocked his view. "What's going on?" he asked. "Maybe we should go down there now."

"Not yet!" said Evie. "I want to hear what Maddy says."

Maddy crossed her arms and looked Mal up and down. "Remember how I told you there were bad eggs in the group? Looks like you just cracked one, Mal." She laughed. "Except I'm not the one who's going to get scrambled tonight. Especially now that we know you don't have any powers after all."

Evie winced.

"What?" cried Carlos. "Are they hurting her?"

"Only with bad puns."

"I knew it! That message was fake! You were just pretending to be good all along." Mal's voice was clear and calm in the dark.

"Good guess, but then why are you here?" sneered Maddy.

"I had to find out for sure," said Mal. "I thought that maybe I still had a friend on the island."

"Friend? Is that what you thought I was? You cut off the heads of my dolls! You put lye in my hair so I had to change its color! You didn't like that everyone called us twins! Some friend you are! You're more delusional than your mother!" shrieked Maddy.

"Ouch," said Evie. "Did Mal really do all those things?"

"Um, yeah," said Carlos. "I mean, she is Maleficent's kid. She was pretty mean growing up."

"And you were telling that goblin back there to fetch the rest of your crew down here so they could ambush me," said Mal.

"Exactly," said Maddy.

The villains crowded around Mal, so that she was pressed against the railing at the edge of the bridge.

"Okay, okay, let's go get her now," said Evie, and they

ran out of their hiding place and headed toward the bridge, Jay in the lead.

"Okay, fine! I was a little brat! I'm sorry, okay?"

"Only suckers are sorry," said Maddy. "And Anti-Heroes are the biggest suckers of all!"

"Don't you get it?" Ginny Gothel asked. "The professor's wrong! There's no hope for us and we don't want any! We're villains at heart! True villains! Not like you!" She raised her fist to the sky. "Evil lives!"

"Evil lives," echoed the Gastons, slapping their fists to their palms.

"When the rest of this pathetic little island discovers their hero was fed to the crocodiles, what do you think will happen to that silly little club?" asked Maddy with a crazed smile. "Everyone will realize that there's no hope in trying to be good! Evil always triumphs! Anti-hero is just another name for villain, and we'll be villains forever!"

"You don't have to do this," said Mal. She'd had to climb on the railing to get away from them, and Ginny was still blocking her way. "It won't prove anything. Maddy, you're not going to get your old hair back, but maybe I can help you fix it. I'm pretty good at spells now."

"Shut up," said Maddy. "And I don't have to do this. I want to!" she shrieked, and the rest of the group joined in her laughter. "Ginny, why don't you do the honors," she offered.

"Let's do it together," said Ginny.

With matching grins, the two of them pushed Mal off the railing and into the bay.

Maddy leaned over the edge. "Say hi to the crocodiles! Tell them dinner's served!"

"Jay! Carlos! Hurry!" cried Evie. "Mal can't swim!"

chapter 32

Unfair Fight

How about that, high heels were finally useful for something, Evie discovered after hitting Ginny Gothel in the back with one. The dark-haired girl screamed and clawed at her, almost scratching her across the cheek.

"Not the face!" cried Evie, furious. "Anywhere but the face!" Ginny lunged for her and the two of them fell to the ground, pulling each other's hair.

Jay took care of the Gastons by running between them at just the right moment so they ended up bumping heads and falling to the ground, moaning. But Mad Maddy and Anthony Tremaine kept from the fray. Carlos knew the Stepmother's grandson would shy away from a fair fight, preferring to have the deck stacked on his side, and it would be easy enough to send Anthony running if he played it right.

"What are you waiting for!" Carlos said, throwing down some judo moves he'd seen in his video games.

Anthony rolled his eyes and took off.

"Well?" Carlos said to Mad Maddy as the Gastons slunk away and Ginny ran off whimpering. "It's only you against the three of us now."

Maddy tossed her bright blue-green hair and sneered, her eyes wide with maniacal fury. "You think you've won here, but I promise you, all of Auradon will burn, just like Camelot!" she said, cackling like a hag as she disappeared into the night.

Evie picked herself off the ground and ran to the railing, scanning the dark water. "Where's Mal?" she asked. "I don't see her!"

"There!" said Jay, pointing to a dark purple head and arms flailing in the waves.

"Dive! What are you waiting for?" Evie asked as Jay hesitated by the rail.

"I can't swim!" he confessed. "It's not like there were lessons on the Isle of the Lost, you know!"

Carlos ran up and began to remove his heavy jacket. "I can dog-paddle! I'll go!"

"Wait!" said Jay. "Crocodiles!"

Mal was surrounded by several of the large scaly beasts

snapping their jaws. She was bobbing up and down in the water and screaming for help.

"We're coming!" said Evie. "Carlos is coming to save you!"

Carlos climbed up on the rail and stared down at the hungry crocodiles. "Um, I am?"

"Go!" said Evie. "Don't worry about the crocs, Jay and I will draw them away!" She gave him a little push and he dropped into the water. She saw his black-and-white head above the waves as he inched his way toward Mal.

"Great! How are we going to do that?" asked Jay.

"With bait!"

"Awesome!" he said. "Wow, you really travel with everything you need, huh?"

Evie gave him a look.

"Hang on, are we the bait?" asked Jay with a groan.

"Yes! Hurry!" Evie threw her other heel so it bounced on the nearest crocodile's head. Then she whistled while dangling a leg over the side of the bridge. "Over here! Yoo-hoo!"

Jay stretched his torso from the edge of the dock and began to wave his arms. "Come on! Over here! Come and get me!" Then, seized by a sudden flash of brilliance, he began to chant. "Tick-tock, tick-tock, tick-tock!" It was common knowledge in the Isle of the Lost that the crocodiles in its waters were no ordinary crocodiles, as they were descended from the one and only Tick-Tock himself. The sound of a ticking clock was almost a lullaby for them, and the crocodiles were hypnotized by Jay's chanting, swimming toward him and Evie.

Mal screamed one last time before disappearing under the water, but in a burst of speed, Carlos was by her side. He dove beneath the waves and hooked his arms underneath hers.

"I've got her! I've got her!" he yelled, keeping Mal's head above the water as he kicked his way back to shore, dodging the crocodiles, which were now circling Jay eagerly, entranced by his rhythmic chanting.

"Tick-tock, tick-tock . . . yeah, that's right, come on over here. Tick-tock, tick-tock," said Jay. "Tick-tock, tick-tock!"

Evie pulled her leg back from the edge and ran to help Carlos, and together they hauled Mal back safely on land.

chapter 33

Serpent's Scales

It was late on Sunday when a fairy tapped Ben on the shoulder and told him that Faylinn had asked that he meet her with her team of archivists in the oak tree's library. Ben had passed the time while waiting by looking over the latest weather reports for the entire kingdom to see if anything had gotten worse. There hadn't been any new sightings of the purple dragon or snake in the last few hours, but who knew when it would strike next.

He followed the fairy up the winding staircase to a massive library housed in one of the topmost branches of the oak tree. Faylinn was flying in front of a huge projection screen, buzzing quietly with her team. The room was cozy and warm, with a crackling fireplace behind a grate, and long tables with pretty intertwined leaves and branches where the fairies worked.

"Ben, you're here, good," she said, flying over to him. "I think we've found something."

She motioned to the images projected on the wall, which showed two blown-up photos of purple scales. Faylinn flew over and motioned to sharp ridges on one of the scales. "Look at this," she said. "The ridges on your scale are almost identical to the one on the right, even though the one on the right is almost ten times its size. The one on the left is your serpent scale, and the other one is about the size of a dragon scale."

"A match, then?" he asked.

"We think so. Either there are two different creatures, with identical ridge patterns, or these scales are from one creature that can take two different shapes. We think it is the latter, as it would be nearly impossible to find two creatures with these specific markings," she said, buzzing between the two photographs.

"Where's the dragon scale from?" he asked, trying not to show how anxious he was. "Is it Maleficent?"

"Not exactly," she said, coming over to fly by his shoulder. Her voice was tiny and sharp as a wind chime.

He exhaled. "What does that mean? What's it from?"

"The scale isn't from any creature we have in our files. As much as we tried, we couldn't find a match, actually, until Lexi Rose remembered we'd received something similar not so long ago." Faylinn clicked to the next slide. "As you know, fairies like to study every aspect of nature, and we ask that if anyone in Auradon discovers something new in the natural world, they send it to us so we can add it to our collection. Recently, a team of dwarfs were digging a new mine down by Faraway Cove, when they came across something unusual."

The other fairies shifted in their seats and looked uneasy as the slide on the screen showed a group of dwarfs mugging for the camera, their wheelbarrows filled with sparkly diamond rocks. "Look over here," she said, flying back to the screen and flitting over the cavern floor.

Ben leaned forward and saw that the ground was littered with the same purple scales.

"The dwarfs closed the mining operation soon after. They said they felt the tunnel was haunted even though they never saw anything, but they sensed a strange presence inside it. One of them—I think it was Doc's nephew—noticed the purple scales and sent a few to the archive."

"Faraway Cove's pretty close to Charmington," said Ben. "And Camelot is directly north of it as well. The dragon must have used these mining tunnels to disappear in and out of sight, which is why Arthur's men could never catch it. I need to take a team into that mine."

"The dwarfs sent a map, so you should be able to find the entrance easily enough," said Faylinn. "I'll have one copied for you."

"Hold on, you still haven't told me—could the scales be Maleficent's?" he asked.

"I'm sorry to tell you it's because we don't know. As it turns out, we don't have a sample from Maleficent. Prince Philip's sword was wiped clean after their battle twenty years ago. But if you can send one from the lizard in your library, then we could tell you for certain."

"Thanks. I'll have my men send over a sample as soon as I can. This has been really helpful." He shook Faylinn's tiny hand with his thumb and forefinger and waved to the rest of the fairies.

"Ben, about this shapeshifting dragon . . . even if it isn't Maleficent, it's still incredibly dangerous. And if it is able to shift in form and size, that means it is capable of incredibly powerful magic. You must be prepared to fight it with similar enchantment. I know the rules of Auradon, so I don't give this advice lightly," she said, buzzing worriedly.

"I won't go alone, don't worry. I'll tell Merlin to meet me at Faraway Cove as soon as possible. And he can bring his wand this time." Ben smiled. "I know he's been itching to use it."

Faylinn nodded. "I can imagine." Seeing the somber look on his face, she buzzed comfortingly by his shoulder.

"Remember, when in doubt, think of happy thoughts and you'll find your way."

He smiled at the tiny fairy. The happiest thought he could think of was Mal and her friends returning safe from the Isle of the Lost. He hoped it would come true.

chapter 34

Underwater Epiphany

"Ugh, the leather is going to shrink," said Mal, wringing her jacket and trying to dry her hair. She had already vomited up a gallon of water, and was still shaking from the near drowning, not to mention the near-crocodile-dinner experience. But Mal being Mal, of course she didn't want to show how shaken she was, so she focused on mourning her ruined jacket instead. "What a bunch of dock rats we are," she said with a laugh. Carlos was similarly soaked to the bone, and Evie was shoeless, her jacket torn. Her bird's-nest hair could rival any of Cruella's fright wigs.

"Speak for yourselves," said Jay, who was dry and without a scratch.

"Don't worry about the jacket, I can make you another one," said Evie, running a brush through her hair and trying to make herself look presentable.

"I shouldn't have run off like that," said Mal. "I'm sorry. I thought Maddy was my friend."

Evie patted Mal on the shoulder; her hand made a wet, squelching sound and she withdrew it in alarm. "Oh, uh, it's okay, we all make mistakes."

"I didn't think she would betray me like that," said Mal. "I really thought she was part of the Anti-Heroes club."

Carlos was sitting on the ground. He'd removed his shoes and socks in an effort to dry them. He pulled seaweed from his hair. "What do you think Maddy meant when she said, 'All of Auradon will burn, just like Camelot'?"

Evie shrugged. "Isn't that what villains do? Threaten?"

"It sounded a little more specific than that, don't you think?" said Carlos. "How did she know about the fires in Camelot, then?"

"Hang on, she said something about Camelot?" asked Mal.

"Yeah, and didn't you say that's where that purple dragon is?" said Carlos.

Mal nodded. "Yeah."

"Maybe Ben put it on the news," said Evie.

"Maybe," said Mal. She shook out her jacket. "Listen, I need to tell you guys something, but we should get cleaned up first, I can't think with all this wet stuff on me." She shook her hair and droplets rained all around. "The Junk Shop isn't far from here, so Jay and Carlos can get cleaned up over there. Evie and I will go back to the Bargain Castle across the street. Meet us there after you get changed."

The four of them walked back into town, Mal squelching with every footstep, Evie walking in stockings, Carlos simply barefoot and holding his wet sneakers, and Jay practically skipping. The boys crossed over to Pity Lane and headed for Jafar's while Mal unlocked the door to the Bargain Castle.

Mal turned to Evie with a wan smile. "By the way, thanks for coming after me."

"You're welcome. It's what friends do," said Evie.

Mal nodded. "Then thanks for being my friend. My real friend."

Later, when the boys arrived, Carlos was dressed in a purple-and-yellow sweater and shorts that were too big for him. Evie was wearing one of Mal's old T-shirts, holey jeans, and a pair of Mal's old boots. The four friends sprawled on the carpet and chairs in Mal's room. Carlos was even able to get a fire going in the fireplace. They hadn't slept all night and it was already close to sunrise.

"Mal, what did you want to tell us earlier?" said Carlos, poking the fire with a stick. He placed his sneakers by the grate, hoping they would dry soon.

"The crocs in the bay," said Mal. "Aren't they usually by Hook's Inlet? Why were they all around Doom Cove all of a sudden?"

"Change of scenery?" snorted Jay.

"No, it was like they were guarding something. Something important," she said, warming her hands by the fire. "I think I know what it is."

"The entrance to the Catacombs," said Carlos promptly.

"Yeah, how'd you know?" Mal asked, looking a bit miffed that a little bit of her thunder had been stolen.

"Lucky guess," said Carlos with a smile. "Seriously, what else could it be?"

"Anyway, when I was underwater, I thought I saw a cave down there. The crocodiles were swimming out of it. It looked like it was their nest."

"Hmm," said Jay. "If the crocodiles were coming out, there must be another entrance from the topside. Crocodiles prefer to make their homes on land, not underwater. Also, if Jafar, Evil Queen, and Cruella did go down there, I doubt they swam. For one, none of them can."

"Perfect," said Carlos. "Because I sure wasn't looking forward to getting wet again. My sneakers just dried."

"We should tell the Anti-Heroes group so they can help

us find it," said Evie. "Yen Sid told everyone to be back at the basement by sunrise, so we'll go and tell them then."

"Good idea," said Jay.

"It's funny," said Mal. "If we're right about this, and that crocodile cave down there is the entrance to the Catacombs, Maddy thought she was getting rid of me, but instead she did us a favor."

"She helped us instead of harming us," said Carlos, putting his dry socks back on.

"It's like Fairy Godmother always says," said Evie, hugging a purple pillow to her chest.

"Don't let the stepsisters get you down?" said Mal.

"Goodness works in mysterious ways. Even in the deepest dark, you'll find a light to shine your way through."

The Four Talismans

"All this has
happened before,
and it will all
happen again."
—Peter Pan

chapter 35

Underground Lair

The anti-heroes were a hardworking bunch, and by noon had combed the entire beachhead, but hadn't been able to find anything. Mal was nearly ready to give up on the search for the tunnel's entrance. After all, she had basically been drowning when she saw the underwater entrance—maybe she'd hallucinated it.

But then, at the very edge of Doom Cove, in a rocky outcropping by the water's edge, Carlos, along with Big Murph, had found a small hole in the ground, about the size of a rabbit burrow.

"That can't be it. How would we fit in there?" Evie asked

doubtfully. "And if it's not big enough for us, it's *definitely* not big enough for a crocodile."

"We dig?" said Jay, who began to shovel away dirt with his hands. "This is the only thing we've seen in hours. We've got to try it." Carlos knelt down to help, and together they were able to make the hole big enough to squeeze through.

Mal knew they didn't need to worry about more crocodiles bothering them now—earlier, she'd sent Hadie to throw a bucket of rotten meat in the water on the other side of the island to draw them away. But as she looked down at the small, dark tunnel ahead, Mal wondered if they had just traded one problem for another. Still, Jay was right. They had to give it a shot.

"Thanks, you guys," Mal called to the assembled team. "I think we've found the entrance. We're going in!"

The sweaty group of anti-heroes cheered.

"Ladies first?" said Jay.

Mal nodded and crawled through the hole. She heard Evie struggling behind, and then the boys. After a few feet, the tunnel widened and they were able to walk upright.

"This better be it," Mal said. "I *really* don't want to be wandering around down here for no reason."

But as they continued down the tunnel, Mal realized she actually felt perfectly at home. The cave was dark and wet and filled with furry things that skittered at the edge of her vision. Why do caves get such a bad rap anyway? What's wrong with a few spiderwebs? she wondered just as she stepped into a giant floor-to-ceiling cobweb. She struggled to push through, only to get more caught up in its lacy white stickiness.

"Don't spiders have anything else to do?" she asked aloud.

Carlos shook his head and helped pull the cobwebs away. They continued on, but stopped again when Evie shrieked at a tiny rodent that had made the mistake of crawling halfway up her pant leg.

"Just tell it to get out of the way," Mal suggested. "Didn't Evil Queen ever teach you how to deal with mice?"

"No, Mom only cared about whether I knew how to line my eyelids properly," said Evie, catching her breath as the small creature scampered off into the crevices.

"Oh, I forgot, I brought something from the Junk Shop," said Jay as he removed a flashlight from his pocket and jiggled the batteries until they came to life. The sudden flood of light illuminated the cavern's interior—a collection of giant cool-looking spiderwebs, slimy wet puddles, and an unexpected item—a gold poison-heart bracelet glittering on the ground.

Evie picked it up. "It's my mom's!" she said excitedly. "They must have been down here! We're going the right way!"

Walking farther on, they discovered other clues. A long cigarette holder that could only be Cruella's, and a few coins that could only have fallen from Jafar's pouch. They kept going, energized by their discoveries, until the flashlight showed a succession of large animal footprints.

"These tracks look too big for crocodiles, right?" Jay asked, inspecting them. "Plus, I think these are paw prints."

"Way too big," agreed Mal.

"Great," said Carlos. "Huge scary monster ahead."

They went deeper into the cave, moving forward cautiously.

Then, from somewhere in the darkness, a faint sound drifted through the cave, almost like the snuffling of an animal of some kind.

"Stop it, Jay!" said Mal, whirling to face him just as he was about to make that snuffling noise again.

"Couldn't resist," said Jay.

He offered Carlos a high five, but Carlos just shook his head. "Not cool, man. Not cool. We need to find the Poisoned Lake," he said, studying one of the maps from Yen Sid. As far as he could tell, the body of water that surrounded the Toxic Tree with the Fruit of Venom should be the first of the underground lands they would pass. "I wonder how the tree can grow. I mean with all this darkness, how can anything live down here?"

"Maybe it feeds on poison from the lake," said Evie.

"For that matter, how can there be a lake underneath the ocean?"

"We're underneath the ocean floor, obviously. Plus,

everything is made by magic down here," Mal said. "Don't you remember?"

"Yeah, I guess so," said Carlos as he stared at the tree. "All the books said that the magic creates the ideal location for each talisman. Okay, let's go this way."

They followed the path as it led them farther down into the earth, so steep at times that they were almost sliding. The tunnel narrowed and then widened again. Some passages were flooded, and they had to roll up their pants to cross. Eventually, the cavern grew so enormous that they could no longer see the top of the cave. They kept walking until the path split in two directions.

Just then, they heard that strange snuffling sound again. Carlos looked petrified, but Mal slapped a hand on Jay's mouth in annoyance. "Stop!"

"Okay, okay, it's hard to resist. It's boring down here," Jay said, his voice muffled behind her hand.

"Where to?" Mal asked Carlos.

Carlos looked down at the map. "It doesn't say." He studied the two tunnels in front of them. One of the paths was covered with the same large tracks they'd noticed earlier, but the other was clear. "I don't know."

"Hmm," said Mal. "The lake is poisonous, right? Whatever lives down here would know that, so instead of following its tracks, maybe we should choose the opposite direction. We need to find the one place the big guy doesn't go."

"Sounds good to me," said Carlos, who wasn't looking forward to meeting a large animal—or whatever it was—underground.

They set off down the undisturbed path. After walking a few feet, the flashlight went out, but Jay knocked it against the stone and it flickered back to life. The cave was smaller here, just big enough for them to pass through.

"I think we're close to water now," said Mal. "The air is damp."

"And that smell," said Evie. "Talk about toxic!" Carlos was already pinching his nose and Mal and Evie did the same. Jay pulled off his beanie and held it over his face. They kept moving, until they heard the sound of water as it washed against sand. It had to be the Poisoned Lake.

They broke into a run, Jay shining the light and pointing it at the end of the cavern.

A large, deep purple lake bubbled with toxic gas. In the middle of the water was a small rocky island where one lone apple tree stood, its fruit ripe and red and luscious. The four of them stared at it, not quite believing what they were looking at. It was impossible to think that anything grew underground, and that, after all that walking, they had actually found one of the most dangerous objects in the world.

"Okay, let's figure out how to get me over there," said Evie, rolling up her sleeves. The fruit was her mother's talisman.

"We need to find a way to make a raft," said Carlos. "Maybe with some of the branches we saw back there, and anything else we can find."

They walked back into the dark tunnel, searching for anything they could use to build a boat, when a strange sound echoed all around, distant but growing louder by the second.

Snuffle, grunt.

Mal ignored Jay. She hated it when he goofed off like that.

Grunt, snuffle.

Much louder now.

Snuffle, grunt.

The snuffling and grunting noise was so loud it was hard to concentrate. Mal had had enough. "JAY! I SAID STOP DOING THAT!"

"Yeah, man," said Carlos as he rolled the map back up and shoved it in his pocket. "Lay off on the sound effects."

"Seriously," said Evie, with a toss of her hair. "You're getting on my nerves."

As they turned around to confront their friend, they realized he wasn't standing behind them anymore. His flashlight was on the floor. "Jay?" Mal called uncertainly.

Jay appeared from the darkness, carrying a bunch of dead branches in his arms. "What?" he asked as the sound grew louder and louder. "I left the light here for you guys."

"Jay's not making that sound!" Evie screamed. "RUN!"

Carlos grabbed the flashlight, and they sprinted back toward the lake. But something was blocking the passage. Something large and hairy with huge fanged teeth.

Snuffle, grunt.

Grunt, snuffle.

chapter 36

Fruit of Venom

The four of them ran from the creature and hid, huddling together in a nearby recess, trying not to make any noise as whatever that thing was that was snuffling and grunting moved away. It sounded awful, like some kind of hideous monster. Evie shivered, hoping it would move away without discovering them. She knew she was first up against her talisman, and wanted to get it over with as soon as she could.

"What is it?" Carlos whispered, shaking.

Mal stuck her head out of the hollow to see if she could see it. "It's big and . . . pink. Like a huge cat, or a tiger, I can't tell."

"A huge pink tiger, great; we're scared we're going to get eaten by a creature that looks like a puff of cotton candy," said Jay.

The snuffling and grunting sound faded.

Evie exhaled. "Okay, let's figure out a way to get across the lake."

Carlos and Jay tried to tie the branches together to make some kind of raft, but it was clear that wasn't going to work as they didn't have anything they could use for twine. Jay kicked at the sad pile of branches dejectedly.

"Let's see how far it is, maybe there's some other way," said Evie.

They entered the larger cavern, which was as big as a professional tourney stadium. Stalactites arched on the ceiling above them, like stars in a black sky. They stared once more at the toxic tree that stood in the middle of a tiny island surrounded by water.

"An island within the island and under water too. Yen Sid is right, the magic down here is wild," said Jay.

Evie stood at the edge of the water, and a smooth rock just large and flat enough to step on appeared. She looked at her friends, who shrugged. She held her breath and jumped on it. Another rock appeared in front of her.

Stepping-stones.

Evie looked over her shoulder and smiled. "Come on, it's like it knows I'm here."

The talismans desire to be found, Yen Sid had told them.

Evie led the way, and the rest followed, careful to make sure they didn't fall into the poisoned water.

"Almost there," said Evie as they stepped closer to the tiny islet holding a single toxic tree. From afar, the tree's knotted bark resembled a pattern of scowling faces.

"Creepy," said Carlos.

"I know," said Mal. "We get to hang out in the coolest places."

"Make sure your feet don't touch the water," warned Evie, who knew a lot about poison, at least when it came to apples. She knew what they looked like, how they smelled, which ones would put you to sleep, and which ones would kill you on the spot. "We'd melt like sugar cubes in a hot cup of tea if you tried to swim in here."

"Nice image," said Jay. "I don't think we'd be as tasty, though."

"We're here!" cried Evie, stepping ashore. She turned around and helped the rest of them onto the island.

"Great, start picking apples!" said Mal.

"Why is it called the Dark Forest," said Jay, looking at the map that Carlos was holding open, "when it only holds one tree?"

"Well, it *is* dark," said Mal. "There's that." The only light came from Jay's flashlight.

"Yen Sid said the maps weren't completely accurate. They were just guesses," Carlos reminded them. From afar, the tree looked small, but up close, it was taller than a building, its trunk as large as a house. It almost took up the entire island.

"I guess I'll have to climb it?" said Evie, staring nervously at the forbidding tree. Evie spent her days indoors, learning how to be pretty. She wasn't really one to climb trees.

The light from the flashlight flickered, growing dimmer by the minute, its batteries fading.

"Hurry, before our light runs out! We've still got three more talismans to recover," said Jay.

"And whatever's out there is still out there," said Carlos. In the distance the sound of faint snuffling echoed in the cave. "Hurry before it finds us."

"All right. I'm going up," said Evie, shaking slightly as she began to climb the tree trunk. She pulled herself up on the nearest branch and started the long, slow climb to the top, where the fruit was. Twice the thorns pricked her, but she ignored the little nicks on her legs and arms. She had work to do, and she could always get rid of them with concealer later.

Down below, her friends waited anxiously, calling up advice. "Watch that branch—go the other way! Get a toehold on the left and lift yourself up!"

When she finally reached the top of the tree, she was stumped. There were hundreds of apples. All of them poisoned, she knew, but there was only one talisman. Only one Fruit of Venom. Which could it be?

"There are a lot of apples up here!" she called down. "I don't know which one to pick . . . they all look alike!"

"You'll know which one!" called Carlos.

Focus! Evie told herself. Her friends were doing their best to help out, and they had to get out of here soon before that snuffling monster returned. Concentrate on the apples. There were so many of them and they were all so red and juicy.

"Which one?" she wondered aloud, and then she saw it through the highest branches.

One golden apple among all of the red ones.

She clambered up and plucked it from its branch. It was gorgeous, shiny, and perfect. Evie was mesmerized by its beauty. It looked absolutely delicious, and it was practically asking to be eaten, what could it hurt, what if she just took one tiny . . .

"What are you doing!" Jay yelled from below.

Too late; Evie had already taken a bite of the apple. It *was* delicious, and for a moment she didn't regret it. Then her eyelids drooped as she yawned.

"Evie! What's happening?" asked Mal.

"I feel . . . sleepy, like the dwarf." Evie laughed as she sat on the branch she'd been standing on, her head beginning to fog from the poison.

"Don't! Stay awake!" cried Mal.

"I'll try!" said Evie. She stood back up, fighting against the urge to sleep. She'd accidentally gobbled a poisoned apple once or twice when she was a kid, so maybe she had some kind of resistance to them. Her mother was always leaving them everywhere.

"I should have known better," she grumbled, already growing weaker and trying to fight off the sleep that was threatening to overwhelm her. "I'm just going to take a little nap, okay?" she called down.

"No!" Mal cried. "No naps! No resting. Just keep moving!"

"Moving," said Evie. "Got to keep moving. . . ." She struggled to keep her eyes open, scrunching her face into odd contortions, holding one lid open with a finger, but it fluttered shut. Evie's knees were wobbling and all she could think of was how nice it would be to lay down her head and take a brief—

"No!" Mal cried, again. Or maybe it was the third time. Evie hadn't realized that she had sat down once more. I'm in trouble, she thought. *Big trouble.*

"Get up!" called Carlos.

Jay was getting ready to climb the tree himself, but when he placed his hands on the bark, a force pushed him away and he flew to the ground.

Only Evie could climb the tree. This was her talisman.

"It says here that only by mastering the Fruit of Venom can you counter its poison," said Carlos, reading from the map. "Evie, don't give in! Save yourself!"

Save myself, but from what? Evie thought, before everything went black and the poison overcame her.

When she opened her eyes, she was standing in a room not unlike her mother's bedroom, on a podium in front of a Magic Mirror.

"Where am I?" she asked. "Where are my friends?"

She was alone. Then she realized—she was alone because they had abandoned her and she had no friends. Every insecure, jealous, and poisonous thought filled her mind.

She was standing before the legendary Magic Mirror, and it looked like it had before it was destroyed—whole and full of evil counsel.

"What's this?" asked Evie.

She stared at the mirror. It showed her Mal and Maddy laughing at her, pointing and screeching, and mocking her.

Mal was never my friend, thought Evie. She was only pretending. The minute Mal returned to the island, she forgot about Evie.

The mirror showed another image: Mal, Jay, and Carlos leaving her alone at the Poisoned Lake. They had left the minute she'd climbed the tree. They were laughing at her, and they were going to leave her to that awful grunting creature. She was alone and she would always be alone.

Mal's mother had exiled her and her mother to the Castle Across the Way. Evie had grown up with only spiderwebs for company. She'd never had friends until the three of them, but maybe she'd never had friends at all.

Maybe it was all a lie. No one liked her. Everyone was only pretending, and now that she knew the truth, she would destroy them all. She would make them *hurt*, she would make sure they never laughed like that again. She would show them what it meant to be alone, and abandoned, and friendless. . . .

Friendless?

Yen Sid's words echoed in her mind. *Evie, remember that when you believe you are alone in the world, you are far from friendless.*

Yen Sid had told her the total opposite of the poisonous thoughts that now filled her brain.

She stared at the mirror and the image of her friends deserting her. It wasn't true. It couldn't be true. Maddy had betrayed Mal, but Mal had never betrayed Evie. Carlos and Jay were like her brothers. The three of them would always be there for her.

"You're wrong!" she cried to the mirror. "My friends are here! They're waiting down there! Waiting for me!"

She stepped away from the mirror, holding the apple in her hand. "I'm not alone! I am far from friendless! I am surrounded by my friends, and I will return to them!"

The mirror shattered and Evie screamed. Suddenly she was on the ground, looking up at the faces of her friends.

"What happened?" she asked.

"You fell," said Carlos. "All the way down, and we couldn't wake you."

"We thought you were going to go to sleep forever, or at least until we could get Doug to come and wake you up with true love's kiss." Mal smirked.

"You okay?" said Jay, helping her up.

Evie nodded, rubbing the sleep from her eyes and tossing back her hair. "I'm awake, at least!" she announced with considerable flair.

"Did you get it?" asked Mal. "The talisman?"

In answer, Evie showed them the golden apple, which was whole once more, but no longer shining. "It totally messed with my head, but I purged the poison from my body and mastered the talisman. Yen Sid was right, we've got to be careful with these things . . . they're tricky."

"What did it do?" asked Mal, curious.

Evie shook her head and placed the apple in her handbag. "Let's just say I knew you guys wouldn't leave me here alone."

Mal rolled her eyes. "Well, one more minute and we might have," she joked. "But then who's going to make my Auradon Prep prom dress?"

"Hey, guys," Jay interrupted. "Look at this." He and Carlos were standing in front of a doorway carved into the tree trunk.

"That wasn't here before," said Carlos.

"And look—the lake is draining!" said Evie. The tiny islet began to shake.

"Now that Evie has the Fruit of Venom, this place is self-destructing!" said Mal.

"Do we open it?" said Jay.

"I don't think we have a choice," said Mal, looking around as the ground rumbled beneath them. It felt like the whole island was about to crumble.

"Let's go, that thing is heading over here," said Carlos, scanning anxiously for any sign of the snuffling beast.

"Open it!" yelled Mal.

Jay threw open the door, and a blazing light shone from the darkness. "It looks like a desert in here!" he told them, stepping inside. Evie and Carlos followed behind.

Mal waited by the entrance, her eyes on the lake, or what was left of it, ready to defend her friends from the mysterious creature in the tunnels.

But the monster never appeared, and so Mal followed her friends through the door in the tree.

chapter 37

Sand Snake

The first thing Jay noticed when he stepped through the tree was how hot it was. He had been shivering in the damp cavern, but now he was almost sweating. Instead of a wet cave, he was standing on a golden desert plain.

Evie followed, but as she crossed the threshold, her knees turned to rubber and she stumbled. Jay caught her and helped her through. "Whoa. That poison must still be working."

She nodded. "I'll be fine in a minute."

Carlos followed, blinking at the unexpected light, with Mal bringing up the rear. When they were all through, the door slammed with a bang and vanished. Carlos unrolled a new map. "This must be the Haunted Desert," he said. "It says the Cobra's Cave is somewhere in the Dunes of Sorrow."

Jay looked around. There wasn't much to see, just a whole lot of desert, and wave after wave of sand dunes. "This must be my territory. It looks a little like what my dad always told me about Agrabah. Although something tells me we won't find any magic lamps, friendly genies, or flying carpets here."

"Too bad. I'd take any of those over that weird pink thing we just avoided," said Mal.

"Any chance the talisman is made of sand?" asked Evie as she scooped up a handful, letting the grains shift and fall between her fingers. "Since that's all there is here."

"Of course it's not made of sand," said Jay.

The wind blew across the dunes, howling like a coyote. But underneath its screech was another sound: a deep, slithering hum.

"There!" said Jay, pointing to a wrinkle in the sand. "It's moving." The wrinkle headed toward them, and the four of them jumped away as it passed directly underneath their feet.

"Maybe your talisman *is* made of sand," said Mal.

"It's not made of sand," repeated Jay, exasperated now.

"That's all I see here," said Mal, refusing to let go of the joke.

"Weren't you listening? Oh, wait, I forgot, you weren't

because you were too busy running after Mad Maddy and getting yourself thrown off a bridge," said Jay. "Yen Sid said it was a Golden Cobra."

He watched the movement in the sand as it slithered away—hold on . . . *slithered?* Before he could explain to his friends, Jay ran after the wriggling line. There was only one thing it could be, and when the line popped out of the dunes, he saw the Golden Cobra rear its ugly head.

The snake hissed, showing its forked tongue. It was the same golden color as the apple Evie had picked earlier.

"I think he's found his talisman," said Carlos as they ran to keep up with Jay, who was chasing the snake.

Jay was fast, but the snake was faster. It slithered across the sand, its golden scales shimmering in the light, while Jay kept stumbling and sinking in the dunes. Jay might be the best runner on the tourney field, but the desert definitely wasn't the ideal location for chasing an evil creature.

The cobra crested a ridge and Jay tried to follow, but when he reached the top, the snake was nowhere to be found.

"Great, it's gone," said Mal, who, along with Evie and Carlos, had been stumbling along after Jay. "What does the map say?"

"It says the Golden Cobra has a cave," said Carlos. "We could check that out, but it doesn't really say where it is."

"Some map," said Mal, crossing her arms across her chest.

They scanned the desert landscape, looking for any sign

of the cobra, but it seemed to have disappeared completely. The heat wasn't helping either, and when the wind picked up, it blew sand at them, clouding their vision and biting their skin like little flies.

"We shouldn't have left for the Catacombs before the maps were done," said Mal, crumpling the piece of paper in frustration.

"We didn't have a choice," said Carlos. "And remember, we've got to find the talismans before our parents do."

"*My* parent is a lizard trapped in a glass-covered pedestal," said Mal.

"Maybe," said Carlos. "Or your parent is a purple dragon that's been plaguing Camelot."

"Guys, stop fighting, it's not helping with my poison headache," said Evie as she massaged her temples.

Mal and Carlos apologized, and the four of them continued to look for any sign of the elusive cobra.

"One good thing about that toxic tree," said Evie. "At least it stayed still."

"There!" Jay yelped. "I see it! I think that's a cave!" He pointed to what looked like a pile of stones in between two dunes in the distance. He ran down the ridge, his friends following behind.

They stood in front of the rocks, which were stacked together tightly. But a small gap between two of the larger ones looked like it could be an opening into a cavern.

"Wonderful, a cave within a cave," said Evie.

"I didn't create this world," said Jay. "You guys coming?"

"Hold on, we need to be careful," said Mal. "Evie was almost poisoned back at the tree and who knows what that snake will do."

"Fine," said Jay.

"Let's go in, but we all stay together," said Mal. "Agreed?"

The others nodded, and they entered the cave. Jay was in the lead, his boots sliding on the sandy floor. He pulled the flashlight out of his pocket and hit the switch, but nothing happened. He tapped it again, and it glowed faintly, illuminating the path before them. A few minutes later, they heard that odd howling noise they'd heard when they first entered the desert.

"Do you think the cobra can make that noise?" Evie whispered.

"I don't know, but I don't really want to find out," Carlos whispered back.

"It's called the Haunted Desert," said Mal. "What do you *think* it is?"

chapter 38

Golden Cobra

"Ghosts don't scare me," Jay said as they kept walking into the darkness with only the sputtering flashlight to light their way. "Hauntings aren't a big deal."

"Oh yeah, what would you know about that?" asked Carlos, trying to get his torchlight zapp to work, but his phone was dead. There had been no time to charge it back on the Isle of the Lost.

"A ghost might try to scare you by rattling his chains or slamming a door shut, but there's nothing to be afraid of. They're basically made of air," said Jay, still following the faint sound of rattling.

"Why do I get the feeling," said Carlos, "that someone is trying to convince himself of something?"

"Because *someone* is totally scared but won't admit it," said Mal, sneaking behind Jay and yelling in his ear. "Boo!"

Jay jumped. "Okay, so I might be little freaked out. But it takes a real man to admit his fears."

"Oh, really," said Mal with a laugh. "It seems to me that just a moment ago you were telling us that ghosts were nothing to worry about."

"So what? Ghosts are the worst, okay? I just wish we could leave this cave already," Jay said.

The howling grew even louder. Carlos plugged his ears and Evie did the same. "Maybe the ghost is deaf?" Mal said. "Why else would it be shrieking at the top of its lungs?"

Jay sighed. "Come on. Let's get this over with." He started to walk faster, but stopped when they reached a sharp corner where the passage was a bit wider. The wind whistled through it, howling and screeching.

"So it's not a ghost after all," said Jay. "It's just the wind flying around these corners. I guess it's like a big flute that plays a note each time the wind blows through."

"Look at Jay, getting poetic on us," said Evie as she, Carlos, and Mal tried to follow Jay into the next passage. But the same force that had pushed Jay away from the tree earlier was acting against them now.

"Wait!" said Mal. "We can't get any farther."

Jay turned around to see his three friends standing at the corner. "I'll meet you back outside. Don't worry about me, I've got this cobra."

"Okay," said Mal, scowling. "I guess we don't really have a choice."

"Remember what Yen Sid said," advised Evie.

"Good luck, man," said Carlos.

Jay promised he would see them soon, and then turned to face the empty tunnel on his own. It wound deeper and deeper into the earth, and the flashlight finally gave out, leaving him in darkness. The howling wind was still kind of scary, but he reminded himself that there was nothing supernatural about it.

At last, he saw a sliver of light at the end of the tunnel, and when he reached it, he discovered it was the entrance to a hidden chamber.

And not just any chamber, but one piled high with gold and treasure. A mountain of shimmering coins reached to the ceiling, so bright it cast its own light around the cavern. Jay had seen such treasure only once before, when he was in the Cave of Wonders in the Forbidden Fortress.

"This isn't real," he said.

Oh, but it issssss, a voice hissed in the middle of all that gold, and Jay looked up to see the Golden Cobra, with its magnificent hood raised around its face, slowly unraveling from a basket. *All this is real, and it could be yours.*

"How?" asked Jay, staring straight into the red eyes of the snake.

I will be your servant, the cobra told him. *I serve the master of the sand.*

Jay was transfixed.

You see that curtain behind you?

Jay turned to see a rich, shining tapestry hanging over the passage he had just come through.

Leave your friends behind and pass through that doorway with me, and you shall have all the riches you desire.

Jay blinked, and suddenly he was seated on a raised platform, wearing a white turban on his head. He was not in the cave at all. He was the Sultan of Agrabah, the richest man in Auradon. Next to him were piles of gold and every kind of precious jewel.

A feast had been set before him with all his favorite dishes, and the people surrounding him bowed, fear in their eyes.

This was what his father had always wanted. His true place in Auradon, above everyone, above everything, wealthy beyond reason, with all the riches of the world at his feet.

All the riches of the world . . .

He blinked against the vision, and returned to the cave, staring at the mountain of gold and the red eyes of the cobra.

What had Yen Sid told him before they had set off?

The riches of the world are all around you.

Jay didn't need much. He wasn't like his father, ruthless and cold. He just liked to play tourney and hang out with his friends. He enjoyed a good game, and good times. Good friends. He thought of how Mal had stood up to her mother rather than let Maleficent hurt any of them. And how Carlos could always be counted on to help with Math Can Be Magic homework, and how Evie would always drop whatever she was doing to listen to him overanalyze an opposing team's play.

He had a great life, and he had wonderful friends. He was already rich beyond measure. The professor was right: the riches of the world were all around him.

"No," he said with a smile.

No? The cobra hissed and flicked its long tongue.

"I'm taking you back to Auradon so you can be destroyed."

The cobra hissed and spat, venom arcing at Jay.

He dodged the poison, and captured the snake with his hand and held it tightly in his grip. The cobra thrashed and hissed, but Jay did not flinch or cower. "You will submit to my will, you are mine to command! And I command you to heel!"

With those words, the cobra stiffened and froze, turning into a simple wooden stick.

When Jay finally emerged from the cave, he found his three friends waiting for him outside. Carlos was reading a book he'd brought, Mal was sketching in her journal, and Evie was combing her hair.

"*That's* the Golden Cobra?" asked Mal, noticing the humble stick Jay was holding.

"It was," said Jay with a triumphant smile. "Okay, where next?"

In answer, the cave behind them began to rumble and disintegrate, just like the tree had done earlier. An outline of a door appeared on one of the rocks that had marked the cave's entrance. Carlos grabbed the knob and yanked the door open, blasting them with cold air. "Let's go!" he yelled.

The three of them followed, Jay using his stick to hold the door open for the girls.

When they reached the other side, after all they had experienced so far, they were only a little surprised to find that they were in a modern city. It was time for Carlos to find his mother's talisman.

chapter 39

Metropolitan Labyrinth

Unlike Auradon City, this city was abandoned and gray instead of bustling with energy and life. Shops and streets were empty, buildings and offices shuttered. The whole place was covered in a thick dark fog, with only a few skyscrapers piercing through the heavy mist.

"Where are we?" said Carlos, his voice shaking slightly. His stomach was churning with the knowledge that this was the home of his particular talisman.

"Some kind of city," said Evie. "It's okay. I don't know about you guys, but I'd rather not see the inside of a cave again. Not to mention sand and snakes."

"Hate to break it to you, but we're still underground in

the Catacombs," said Mal, but even she looked relieved to be somewhere that resembled the real world.

"Magic created all this?" asked Evie. "Buildings and everything? That's pretty crazy."

Mal knocked on a brick wall. "Yeah, and it's real too."

Jay turned around in a circle, looking up at the tall buildings. "Interesting."

"All right, enough sightseeing. We've got to keep going," said Mal. "What does the map say?"

"It says Cruella's talisman is in the House of Horrors," said Carlos, checking the map.

"I thought your house was called Hell Hall?" said Evie.

"Yeah, and it sure was a house of horrors," said Carlos. "I think we go that way." He headed east.

"What does the ring look like?" asked Mal.

"It's the big green one Cruella used to wear," said Evie. "It's pretty, actually. You think Carlos might give it to me instead?"

They walked past houses and buildings, but all of the doors were closed, curtains drawn. The entrance they'd used to enter this world was still open behind them. Through it Carlos could see just a little bit of the sandy desert, and he considered running back there. Retrieving his mother's tallisman wasn't exactly high on his list of favorite things to do.

The four of them walked down the center of the road. Just like the other two worlds, this one was empty. There were no people here; the entire place was quiet, a mere facade. Not a real city at all but a place held together by magic—a home for the talisman. He led them right, then left, then two rights, and he stopped, confused.

"Wait, that's the door to the desert again," Carlos said. "We're walking in circles."

"No, we're not," said Jay. "If we had walked in circles we would have only made right turns. I definitely recall a left."

They set off again, this time turning left, left, then right, then left, then right again. But once more, they came to the same doorway.

"Think we're in some kind of magic maze?" Mal asked. "Let me guess: the map can't help us."

Carlos checked, looking at the map from different angles. "Actually, according to the map, the house should be right here, where we're standing. I'm not sure what's going on, if the landscape is shifting so it doesn't match the map, or I'm reading it wrong."

"At least we have the door to the desert," said Jay. We can always go back the way we came. . . . Why are you looking at me like that?"

Carlos pointed. The door wasn't there anymore.

"We're trapped!" yelped Evie.

"And it doesn't seem to want us to find what we're looking for, and it doesn't look like there's a way out of here," said Mal.

"Maybe it'll appear. I don't know how magic works. Let's keep walking," said Carlos.

"In circles?" asked Jay.

"You have a better idea?" asked Mal.

"I guess not," Jay admitted. "Okay, carry on, circles are fine."

"Maybe if we keep walking we'll see something else," said Carlos.

They kept going, looking for the house, and once again they ended up where they began. "Hold on," said Carlos. "I think the map is right. The House of Horrors *is* right here."

"But these are all regular buildings, not mansions," said Evie. "I don't see Hell Hall anywhere."

"The talisman isn't in Hell Hall, I made a mistake," said Carlos, pointing to a dusty window that had been right in front of them all along. He hadn't noticed it because he had assumed that the "House of Horrors" was his mother's house. This was a fur shop, and in the corner was a sign that read HOUSE OF HORRORS. SALE TODAY!

"I think I'm supposed to do some shopping," said Carlos.

"Well, go on, then," said Jay.

"I'm going! Give me a sec," said Carlos.

But he didn't move. He couldn't.

"Come on, man, just do it. You know you can. Go!" said Jay, giving him a little push.

Finally, Carlos opened the door and looked over his

shoulder. “You guys probably can’t come in, can you?” he asked hopefully. But sure enough, when Mal, Evie, and Jay tried to follow, they were barred from entering.

“We’ll wait here,” said Evie.

“Good luck,” said Mal. “You’ll need it.”

“Bring back that ring soon. I’m getting hungry,” said Jay.

Carlos swallowed his fear, squared his shoulders, and walked inside.

chapter 40

The Ring of Envy

The House of Horrors didn't live up to its name at all, for when Carlos stepped inside, he found it was an elegant fur shop. The room was decorated in the manner of a fabulous salon, with racks and racks of elegant fur coats everywhere. There were fox chubbies, sable throws, mink stoles, floor-length trenches, and fur-trimmed opera capes. White Mongolian vests, black goat-hair ponchos, cozy raccoon cocoon coats, cheetah-print boleros, and silver-tipped mantles.

There was an elevator at the back of the store, and he walked toward it, as if drawn there by an invisible cord. The doors opened silently and he entered, his hand pulled to the button for the topmost floor.

When Carlos stepped out of the elevator, he was no longer inside a fur shop. Instead, he was walking through a mist, a gray cloud that covered everything. In the distance, he saw a green light blinking.

He walked toward it, his heart thudding in his chest, hoping he wouldn't chicken out. The youngest of the group, Carlos was often worried that while he was smart enough, he wasn't as brave as the others were. It had taken a great force of will to enter the House of Horrors alone.

The mists parted and he saw the ring at last. It was indeed as large as a quail egg and as green as a spring meadow. And it was Cruella de Vil's ring all right, because she was wearing it.

Carlos stepped back with a yelp.

"Hello, darling," his mother said, blowing a cloud of smoke in his face. "Looking for this?"

"You found it?" he asked. "You found your talisman?"

"Well, of course I did, child! It's mine!" she screeched.

He was too late, Carlos realized. Cruella already had her ring.

"Shoo, boy, don't you know when to leave your mother alone?" sneered Cruella.

Carlos backed away, petrified. He had failed his friends, and he had failed Auradon. But even as he beat himself up, he remembered Yen Sid's words. *You possess a keen intellect;*

however, do not let your head rule your heart. Learn to see what is truly in front of you.

Everything in his brain told him to run from his mother, that she had already captured the talisman. There she stood, hitching her furs across her shoulders, glaring at him.

Cruella had always haunted his nightmares, with her crazed declarations and frenzied hysterics. What was truly in front of him? What didn't he see? What was he missing?

His head screamed at him to run. . . .

But his heart . . . His heart told him to stay and fight, that even if he was deathly afraid, he had to find a way to get the ring away from her. He had to prove to himself that he was brave enough, and that he *was* enough.

"Still here? Go and tell your friends to leave this place forever," ordered Cruella.

"No," said Carlos. "Not without that ring."

Gathering the last of his courage, he tackled his mother and struggled for the ring, finally pulling it off her finger and placing it on his own.

He felt the rush of power from the talisman shoot through him.

Cruella cackled with glee. "Go ahead, then, use it on me. Destroy me. With that ring you can obliterate me forever. Tell me to throw myself off this roof and I'll do it. Isn't that what you want? Isn't that what you have always wanted?"

Carlos felt the ring throb in his hands. He could destroy

his mother, rid the world of another villain, and stop having nightmares once and for all.

"Do it!" Cruella cackled. "Do it, boy!"

He raised his hand, pointing the ring right at her. Then he dropped his arm down with a sigh. "No, I can't. I'm better than that," Carlos said, turning on his heel and heading for the elevator. *I'm better than you, Mother. No matter what you've always told me.*

Suddenly he was standing outside the House of Horrors, and Jay, Mal, and Evie were looking at him, concerned.

"What happened?" he asked.

"You came out of the building in a trance," said Mal.

"The ring . . ." Carlos muttered. He opened his fist. The jewel had turned a dull green, its power abated for now. "It wanted me to destroy her," he said. "But she wasn't actually there. It was just a vision, just the ring trying to scare me, to make me mad."

"Yep, sounds about right," said Jay. "These talismans must get more power that way."

Carlos nodded and put the ring away in his pocket. Three down. One Dragon's Egg to go.

They looked around for a hidden doorway, but found none. "We could try this," said Carlos, motioning to the revolving door that led back to the House of Horrors. "It's the only door around here that's open. It might be the only way out of here. And from the looks of it, the city is melting!" He yelped as the sidewalk beneath them began to crack.

"Let's go!" yelled Mal. She rushed through the revolving door, and the rest of them hurriedly did the same.

chapter 41

Dragon's Nest

When she pushed through the door, Mal wasn't in the House of Horrors. She wasn't even in a city anymore. Instead, a dark, foreboding mountain loomed in the distance. Lightning crackled in the sky and vultures circled above.

"Maleficent Mountain," she said, when the rest of the team arrived. "Over there." According to the map, Doom Crag lay at the very top of the mountain, where a dragon had made its nest.

"Ouch, that looks like a climb," said Jay.

"You guys know the drill. Only I have to go," said Mal. "Don't worry."

"No," said Carlos. "We'll all go. Remember what the professor said? You don't have to do this alone."

"But this is my talisman," said Mal. "And all of you had to get yours alone."

"We're going with you," said Evie. "At least until the talisman stops us. No arguments."

"You're not getting rid of us," said Jay. "That's how this whole 'having friends' thing works, remember?"

"Fine," said Mal. "Let's go, then."

They trudged through the dead land, air thick with smoke. Sizzling green slime bubbled through cracks in the dirt, and they helped each other over the acrid puddles. Mal soldiered on as Evie groaned and complained that her head still hurt from the poison, and Jay was subdued, probably thinking of the riches he'd rejected. Carlos was definitely still shell-shocked from seeing his mother; real or not, that woman was terrifying.

They were united in their silence. The Dragon's Egg was the greatest of all the talismans and its mistress would have the forces of hell at her command.

"You know, the Dragon's Eye in the scepter isn't an actual eye. It just looks like one. It's really a dragon's egg," said Mal.

"Why isn't it called the Dragon's Egg scepter, then?" asked Carlos.

"Duh, because Dragon's Eye sounds way cooler," said Jay.

"Yeah, I guess so," said Carlos.

"So is there a dragon here?" asked Evie, looking around fearfully.

"Let's hope not," Carlos said.

"You guys can wait here," said Mal. "The mountain won't let you any closer than this."

She began to climb, reaching for a foothold and pulling herself up.

But when Jay put a hand on the mountainside, it didn't push him away, and it didn't reject Carlos or Evie either. When Mal looked down, she was slightly disappointed to find they were climbing right behind her.

Is it because the talisman thinks I'm weak? she wondered.

With that disconcerting thought, she kept climbing, her friends right behind her.

chapter 42

Dragon's Egg

When they reached the top of Doom Crag, they discovered the dragon's nest was the size of a small boat. Its burned and blackened branches were twisted and packed tightly, and there was no sign of an egg anywhere. Mal began to search, getting down on her knees, and the rest of the team did the same, combing through every inch of the foul space.

"It's not here," said Mal, frustrated.

"It has to be," said Evie.

"Maybe they got here before us and found it. Cruella, Jafar, and Evil Queen, I mean," said Jay. "They are supposed to be wandering around down here in the Catacombs, right?"

"Maybe that's why we were all able to climb the mountain," said Mal. She'd scratched her palm on the way up, and she pinched it, trying to stop the blood. "Because the talisman's gone."

"No!" said Carlos. "It has to be here. If they'd found it, this mountain wouldn't be here. Remember what happened in the other places? They started to disintegrate once we recovered the talismans. Keep looking."

Mal searched again, but bumped into Evie, who fell back on Carlos, who tripped over Jay. "There's not enough space for all four of us," Mal complained. "You guys need to leave. You're not helping. Maybe it won't show itself to me because you're all here," she said crossly.

"Are you sure?" said Evie.

"I'm sure," said Mal.

"Fine," said Jay. "If she doesn't want us here, we don't need to be here. And this place gives me the creeps."

"But the professor said . . ." Carlos began.

"He's not here now, is he? He's not the one who had to climb this mountain and look for this egg. Get out of here!" Mal shouted.

Carlos, Evie, and Jay exchanged looks with each other. Mal glared at them until, one by one, they climbed out of the nest and began to make their way down the mountain.

Mal didn't need anyone, she never had. Okay, maybe the four of them had stood together when Maleficent was defeated, but come on, in the end, everyone knew that it was Mal's will that had broken her mother's and reduced the dragon to the size of a lizard.

Although Mal's heart felt small right then, thinking of her friends descending the mountain without her, she couldn't let it stop her. She covered every inch of the nest, and on the third time through the muck, she saw something out of the corner of her eye. Something small and purple.

"Aha!" she said, reaching for it. But Mal had been expecting a green egg, like in the Dragon's Eye scepter. Why was this one purple?

Only when it hatches does it turn green, a voice answered, as if it could read her thoughts. *The Dragon's Egg does not birth a dragon, but a weapon.*

Okay, whatever, thought Mal, stuffing the egg in her jacket. At least that was done. She'd recovered her talisman just fine without anyone's help. Maybe the professor was wrong about her quest; after all, the old guy didn't know everything, right?

She stood at the edge of the nest, ready to head down, when a vulture shrieked from above. She startled, losing her balance, and fell over the edge, just barely holding on to a branch at the very bottom of the nest. Her legs kicked wildly in the air.

Great, she was about to fall off a cliff, and she'd gotten rid of the only people who could have helped her. Why did she always insist on doing everything alone?

Her hands were starting to burn.

She was an idiot, that's why, and she couldn't hold on much longer!

You've held on this long, haven't you?

She had the blood of a dragon, just like her mother.

Don't you?

Her fingers felt like they were starting to fall off.

She was Mal, daughter of Maleficent. Her mom had given her only part of her name, saying she hadn't earned the rest of it yet. But maybe she didn't want her full name at all. Maybe she didn't want to be Maleficent. Maybe she was completely fine with just being herself, being Mal.

Aren't you? Isn't that the whole point?

Who else are you supposed to be?

One hand slipped off the branch, and dirt began falling into her eyes as the roots tore off from the cliff.

Maleficent would never admit to needing or wanting anyone, and had been transformed into a lizard because she didn't have enough love in her heart. But Mal was not her mother. While she was stubborn, and way too proud, she was very different from Maleficent. And right now she wasn't ashamed to admit when she was wrong.

Now she was only holding on by one hand. The branch

was ripping out of the cliff face. She could be falling in moments.

You're wrong. You've never been more wrong—

Evie, Jay, and Carlos needed to discover their own strength and so they had to face their quests for their talismans alone. Mal didn't have to be tested that way, because she already knew that she was strong. But what she didn't know until now, dangling over the edge, was that as strong as she was, she could always use a hand.

Literally.

Maybe that was my test after all—

Strength didn't have to mean facing danger alone. Strength came from trust, and friendship, and loyalty. Plus, Yen Sid was right, this wasn't just her burden to bear, it was theirs too. She hoped her friends were still there.

"You guys! Help!" she yelled. "I need help!"

She kept screaming until she saw their faces peering down at her from the nest above. "Mal! We're coming!" said Evie.

Carlos held Evie's feet as she was lowered down, with Jay as the anchor. Ever so slowly, and ever so carefully, they dragged Mal back to safety.

Mal could barely catch her breath, and her throat still hurt from screaming. Her hands were cut and scratched.

But she was alive.

"Thanks, guys. For saving my life and everything."

"Did you find the egg?" said Carlos, when they were all back inside the nest again.

Mal held up the purple oval that was hard as stone. "Yep."

"Why is it purple?"

"It still has to hatch," said Mal. "But let's get out of here before this mountain completely collapses or something."

As if it heard her, the mountain began to rumble and shake, slowly disappearing back into nothingness now that its purpose had been served and its talisman taken.

chapter 43

Which Witch?

No new doorway appeared in the side of the mountain after Mal had retrieved the Dragon's Egg. She was still a bit dazed from the near-death experience as they climbed back down the mountain.

"How do we get out of here?" asked Evie nervously.

"I think we have to go through *that*," said Carlos, motioning to a cavern at the base of the mountain after consulting the map. "There's no way back, so we'll have to keep going forward."

"Great, another dark tunnel," said Evie, who had just about had her fill of the underground catacombs.

"But I think this one leads us back home, to Auradon," said Carlos hopefully. "If the map is right . . ."

"Let's go," said Mal, who'd found her voice. She held the small purple egg in her fist, unwilling to put it away in her pack just yet.

"Flashlight's dead, so we'll have to feel our way in the dark," said Jay, tossing the torch into a bubbling green puddle with a sigh.

"Then we'll do this the only way we can," said Mal. "Together." The four of them held hands and entered the foreboding cavern.

They'd traveled for a while when the path before them began to shine, and when they rounded the corner, they saw abandoned wheelbarrows and uncut rocks with diamonds still embedded in their core.

"Looks like a dwarf mine," said Evie. She'd seen them in Doug's ZapChats.

"Abandoned," said Jay, picking up one of the shiny rocks.

"Wonder why?" said Carlos. "Looks like they left in a hurry."

"Who knows," said Mal. "Let's keep going."

They kept walking, until Mal suddenly stopped.

"What?" asked Carlos.

"I heard something . . . like footsteps. Can you hear it?" she asked.

Jay listened, absentmindedly pocketing one of the gems on the floor. "Yeah."

"There's someone else here," said Mal.

Evie looked over her shoulder. "Following us?"

"Maybe," said Mal. "Be ready."

"You don't think it's *them* . . . ?" said Carlos, who really had no desire to see his mother right now.

"Who else?" said Mal. "Yen Sid said they're lost down here. Maybe they saw us and now they want to get their talismans back."

"Dad!" Jay called into the darkness behind them. "Are you there?" His voice echoed around the cavern. *Dad, Dad, Dad, Dad.*

No answer, so they kept walking, but the feeling that someone or a group of someones was in the tunnel with them remained. And their hearts dropped when they noticed a few things in the mine—a tube of red lipstick, a fluff of black-and-white fur, and a discarded velvet money pouch. The villains were somewhere close by, and Mal, Evie, Jay, and Carlos were ready to hear Cruella de Vil's sneer or smell Evil Queen's perfume or feel Jafar tap them on the shoulder at any moment. They tried to pretend it didn't bother them a bit, trying to act tough, even as they inadvertently huddled closer together.

"Aieee!" Carlos cried as he bumped into Jay, who yelped as he collided with Evie, who screamed as she fell on Mal.

"It's just us!" said Mal. "Everyone calm down!"

They kept moving, until they heard the footsteps again, louder this time, along with voices. But they must have been coming from the other way—ahead of them rather than behind.

"Who's there!" called Mal while the three others huddled behind her.

"The mine starts down here," they heard someone grumble. "Are we sure this is necessary?"

"Let's just see how deep it goes, and where it leads. It couldn't hurt," said another.

A sudden beam of light flooded the mine shaft, and they blinked, blinded. But even without seeing who it was, Mal knew that voice immediately.

"Ben!" she cried, running toward the group heading down the mine shaft.

"Mal? Is that you?" asked Ben, shining his flashlight her way.

"It is! It's all of us!" she said, appearing out of the darkness.

"You're all right!" he said, beaming as he scooped her up in his arms.

Mal closed her eyes and hugged him back tightly. There was nothing like almost rescuing an entire kingdom—and almost plunging to your death along the way—to make a person appreciate a good hug.

"What are you doing down here? Where did you come from?" she asked.

"I'll tell you everything," he said, at the same time as she said, "I have so much to tell you!"

They laughed as Carlos, Jay, and Evie joined them, a little dirty and smudged, but whole. Ben didn't let go of Mal as he shook the boys' hands and slapped them on the back before giving Evie a quick hug. The five of them grinned at each other.

The old man behind Ben cleared his throat. "Uh, right," Ben said, blushing as he backed away from Mal. "This is Merlin, and you know Grumpy."

The wizard nodded in greeting and the dwarf grunted. "Do you know my son, Gordon? He's at Auradon Prep with you all," said Grumpy.

"We know Doug," said Evie, smiling.

Grumpy huffed. "Everyone knows Doug. Just like his father, too popular."

Evie had to giggle at that.

Ben explained how the Neverland fairies had helped them track purple dragon scales to this deserted diamond mine. Mal's group told them about their journey to recover the talismans.

"So Yen Sid was right, the Catacombs go all the way to Auradon," said Carlos.

"We were just at Maleficent Mountain," said Mal. "There was a dragon's nest on the top of Doom Crag, but we didn't see a dragon back there."

"We're closer than we've ever been, then," said Ben. "The

creature must live here, and it's been getting to Auradon through this tunnel."

Just as he spoke, a fine purple mist covered the cavern, and everyone froze.

"It's here," said Merlin. "The creature is here. Show yourself!" The wizard held his wand high.

"Come out, come out, wherever you are!" said Mal.

"I am King Ben of Auradon and I command you to reveal yourself to us!" said Ben.

The purple mist began to take shape . . . but instead of a fire-breathing dragon or a giant snake, there was only an old witch with purple hair standing in front of them when the mist cleared.

"Madam Mim!" exclaimed Mal, completely shocked to see Mad Maddy's grandmother, and yet something else about her was oddly familiar.

"Hello, dearie!" said Madam Mim with a cheerful wave.

"You know her?" asked Ben.

"From the Isle of the Lost," said Mal.

"Well, I certainly know her. Hello, old friend," said Merlin grimly. "I thought I might see you here, Mim. Up to your old tricks, are you? I'm sorry to say that your mischief ends now."

Madam Mim only laughed, and her cackle echoed throughout the dark cavern. "Oh, I don't think so, you geezer, I'm having way too much fun!"

chapter 44

Wizards' Duel

As she laughed, Madam Mim turned into a large purple dragon. But unlike Maleficent's fierce dragon form, Madam Mim's looked almost comical. Her messy purple hair was still perched on top of her head, and her wings looked the size of a bird's. How on earth did Ben ever mistake this dragon for Maleficent?

"You thought this was my mother?" Mal asked him, rolling her eyes.

Ben laughed nervously. "She was up in the sky, it was hard to see. I don't know, blame magic?"

Still, the group scrambled away as Merlin rolled up his

blue wizard sleeves. He zapped his wand at her, launching sparks, but Mim was too fast. She turned into a fox and scuttled into the darkness. Merlin sent another spell from his wand, but he was too late. Mim turned once more, this time into a raging rhinoceros.

"The boulders!" said Mal, pointing to the giant stones at the top of the mine shaft.

Jay and Carlos ran in front of the animal, pushing the rocks right into the rampaging rhino's path. But just as she was about to be crushed, Mim turned into a crafty hen and flew out of the way.

"Where'd she go?" asked Ben.

"Don't know," panted Mal. "But at least now we know that Camelot's dragon wasn't my mom."

"For sure," said Ben.

Mim must have discovered the entrance to the Catacombs, thought Mal, and she was using it to get her revenge on Merlin, who had bested her during their last battle by giving her the pox. The loony old witch was having fun wreaking havoc in Camelot and stealing food from Auradon. She must have told her granddaughter what she was doing. It's a wonder Maddy hadn't tried to escape to Auradon herself. Maybe she'd been too scared about getting lost down there; she knew the dangers from being in the Anti-Heroes club.

"Mmm, you look tasty!" Mim cackled as she turned into a crocodile and opened her jaws wide.

"GAH!" said Carlos as they ran away from her snapping teeth. Mim reared on her hind legs, her purple hair falling into her face.

"It was you!" cried Mal. "That pink-and-purple thing we saw in the tunnels earlier!"

"Cotton-candy tiger?" said Jay. "I take it back, she's definitely scary!"

They barely got away from her, but Merlin soon came to their rescue. "You're surrounded, Mim!" said Merlin, waving his wand. "The only way out of this tunnel is through me. Your place is on the Isle of the Lost! Surrender!"

"Never!" Mim shrieked, turning back into the fat purple dragon, fire spewing from her mouth. "I'll never go back there! You can't make me!" She shot a fireball at him, but Merlin transformed into a blue sparrow and flew away from her. But Mim deftly conjured a cage, trapping him.

"Some powerful wizard!" scoffed Mal. "Can't he turn into something . . . I don't know . . . scarier?"

"I read the history of Camelot," said Carlos. "And when he battled Mim back when Arthur was a kid, Merlin did the same thing—Mim turned into ferocious creatures but Merlin fought her by turning into small and seemingly helpless animals like a rabbit and a turtle. Maybe it's the way his magic works?"

There was no time to discuss further, as Mim was headed their way, ready to spew another fireball.

"No!" cried Ben, rushing forward, but Mim swatted

him with her tail and he was thrown hard across the cavern, hitting the ground with a thump.

"BEN!" cried Mal. She started to run toward him, but Mim stomped in front of her, blocking the way. Then the dragon pushed forward, pressing Mal, Jay, Evie, and Carlos against the wall.

There was nowhere else to go.

"What do we do?" cried Evie. "She's going to roast us!"

"Talismans?" said Jay. "If we use them to hurt someone, I have a feeling they'll come to life again! I can use my cobra staff to hypnotize her!" he said, shaking his wooden stick.

"Or my ring to make her do what we want," said Carlos.

"Poison is always good," said Evie, removing the golden apple from her purse.

"Mal, you've got the Dragon's Egg," said Carlos. "You could command all the forces of hell."

"Not until it hatches," said Mal. "And the only way for it to hatch is if it sits under a dragon."

"You mean you have to put it under Maleficent?" asked Evie.

"Maybe?" said Mal.

"Weird," said Jay.

"But we have ours. Let's use ours," said Carlos, rather desperately, as Mim drew closer.

"No!" said Mal. "We can't use our talismans! Don't you see that's what the evil in them wants us to do? If we use them like this, it would only make their power stronger.

We'd be drawn to the magic . . . and we'd turn into our parents."

"You're right," said Evie, putting away her talisman reluctantly as the boys agreed.

"Then brace yourselves," said Carlos, "and prepare to be roasted."

The four of them huddled together, seeking comfort in each other before the end, and the purple dragon reared back and opened its mouth. But before it could set them on fire, Ben appeared, holding a sword to the dragon's heart.

"Recognize this?" he asked. "Artie loaned it to me; he thought I might need it."

"Excalibur!" cried Carlos, who recognized the sword from Auradon's history books.

"The one and only," said Ben, still facing Madam Mim. "The most powerful sword in Auradon. You know what it can do."

"So I suggest you save yourself the pain, Mim," said Merlin, who had gotten out of the cage by turning into a caterpillar and was now back to being a wizard.

The purple dragon snorted as Ben pressed the blade against its chest. Finally, it turned into a fine purple mist, and Mim was a hag once again, her shoulders slumped. "I'll miss Auradon so," she said. "The sheep were tasty."

"But alas, Auradon is not the place for you," said Merlin. With a wave of his wand, Madam Mim was sent back to the Isle of the Lost.

"Say hi to Maddy for me!" said Mal.

"We need to close this tunnel so that no one else can use it to escape into Auradon," said Ben.

"My thoughts exactly," said Merlin, and with another wave of his wand, the passage behind them was closed forever with an impenetrable wall that no one and no magic would ever be able to breach. "There, it's permanently sealed. No one from the Isle of the Lost will ever be able to use it again."

"Let's go home," said Ben, reaching for Mal's hand.

"Sounds like a good plan," said Mal, squeezing Ben's hand tightly. "You guys ready?"

The other three nodded.

"About time," said Jay. "We've got class tomorrow."

"And homework tonight," said Carlos.

"I hope our feeds updated correctly," said Evie. "Right now we're all supposed to be in bed, sneezing from the flu."

"Did someone say Sneezy? I'm Grumpy," said Grumpy.

"Merlin?" asked Ben. "Do you mind giving us a lift? Just this once?"

"If you could send me back to the Enchanted Wood," said Grumpy, "it would save me a carriage ride."

"I'll be heading back to Camelot myself," said Merlin as he shook everyone's hands.

"You make a good king, Ben," said Merlin. "And you were right in the end, we didn't need magic to capture the dragon. Only diligence and courage, as you have shown."

"Thank you," said Ben. "That means a lot, coming from you. Although we did need magic to send her back to the Isle of the Lost, and to close that passage. And to go home."

"Details, details," said Merlin with a smile. "Who reads the fine print these days?"

"Will you give this back to Artie for me?" asked Ben, handing Merlin the sword.

"With pleasure," said the old wizard with a smile.

"Bye, Merlin," said Mal, and the rest of the group waved.

"Can we get going already?" asked Grumpy.

Merlin rolled up his sleeves. "Return everyone here to where they need to be," said the wizard. Raising his wand for the last time, he sent them all back to where they belonged.

chapter 45

Happily Ever After, for Now at Least

It was Sunday afternoon when they returned to school; the practice fields were quiet and empty, and students were taking advantage of their free time to read under the trees or lazily throw Frisbees across the lawn. Mal blinked at the sudden brightness and serenity, a stark contrast to the dark mine they'd just left. She was still holding the Dragon's Egg tightly in her hand. She was about to put it away when she noticed something—at the edge of the purple was just a hint of green.

The Dragon's Egg births a weapon. The most powerful talisman. Mal shuddered and stuffed the egg back in her pocket for now.

"Home safe," said Ben. He thanked Mal, Jay, Carlos, and Evie for all their help, but he had to go back and meet with his councillors to update them on everything that happened.

"See you in a bit," he said, giving Mal's arm a squeeze.

"Not if I see you first," said Mal, returning his smile.

Ben headed over to Beast Castle as they made their way back to the residence halls. It was almost impossible to believe they had been gone for less than a day, and the weekend wasn't even over yet. It felt like they'd been in the Catacombs of Doom for a lifetime.

"Well," said Carlos. "I guess that's it for now."

"Not quite," said Mal. "We still need to figure out how we're supposed to get rid of these talismans."

Jay nodded. "Tomorrow."

"I need a nap." Evie yawned.

As they strolled back to the residence halls, they saw Audrey and Chad having a picnic under a tree while Jordan and Jane lounged on towels nearby. The Auradon kids waved when they saw them, and they stopped to say hello.

"Hey, Jay," said Chad. "Sorry about . . . um . . . what happened with your eye the other day. And good game yesterday."

"No worries, man," said Jay. The two shook hands and Mal was just a tiny bit disappointed that Jay didn't jump at the opportunity to steal Chad's rather shiny wristwatch.

"Are you feeling better?" Jane asked Carlos worriedly. "You looked so sick at the dance last night."

"Much better," said Carlos, blushing. "Thanks."

"Oh, Jordan," said Jay. "About what happened in your lamp the other day, with the limousine keys. Sorry about that. I returned them to Ben, though."

"It's all right," said Jordan. "I figured you must have needed them badly enough if you had to wish for them."

"See you guys later," said Mal. Evie looked like she was going to fall asleep standing up, and gave a limp wave with her fingers.

"I'm going to stay a bit," said Carlos, taking a seat on a towel next to Jane.

"Me too," said Jay, who was already lounging next to Jordan's towel.

Mal and Evie exchanged meaningful smiles, but didn't tease the boys. They'd save that for later. When they arrived in their room, both of them collapsed on their beds and slept until the alarm woke them up for school the next morning.

Before Mal headed to her classes, she had one more thing to do. She skipped breakfast and went straight to the room at the back of the library. The guards at the door didn't recognize her, and there were a lot more of them this time.

"I need to get in there to see my mother!" she demanded.

"Sorry, King Ben said absolutely no visitors."

"But I will make an exception this time," said Ben,

who had heard the ruckus and walked over to see what was happening.

"You're up early," said Mal.

"Tourney practice. Playoffs are next week," said Ben. "What's up? You wanted to see your mom?"

"Yeah," said Mal.

"Let her through," said Ben.

The two of them went inside, and Mal couldn't help running ahead. She skidded to a stop in front of the domed pedestal.

Maleficent was missing.

The lizard was gone.

And there were only three people who could have taken her.

She gasped. Somehow, the villains had gotten past the guards! "What are we going to do?"

But Ben didn't look alarmed. Instead, he looked sheepish and a bit embarrassed. "Mal, I have to show you something," he said. He brought up a screen on his phone, which showed a lizard in a similar domed pedestal. "That's a live feed."

She looked at it. "But how? But that's . . ."

"Maleficent. When I returned from Camelot, I had her moved from the library to the museum just in case someone tried to do something funny. She's been there the whole time. She hasn't changed or transformed at all, and she's safe."

"But all the guards?"

He looked abashed. "They're there for show, but there's nothing to guard."

"And mother's still just a lizard," Mal said with a laugh.

"Just a lizard." Ben smiled.

Later that day, Ben asked the four villain kids to meet with him to discuss the problem of the talismans. "Obviously, we can't have them around," he said.

"Yes, we have to neutralize them," agreed Mal. "But how?" Where could they find magic powerful enough to purge the talismans of evil? And she still had to figure out how to hatch her Dragon's Egg. She'd peeked at it this morning, and it was definitely starting to glow green at the edges.

"Shall we ask Merlin?" said Carlos.

"The three good fairies?" said Jay.

"Neverland, for sure," said Evie.

But Ben surprised them. "No, I think the person we're looking for is right here."

"Fairy Godmother," said Mal. "Of course!" It was her magic that had collected all the villains of the land and trapped them in the Isle of the Lost in the first place. The most powerful sorcerer in Auradon was their chubby-cheeked middle-aged headmistress, who preferred to teach children how to live *without* magic, but she would know what to do.

"She'll be back from Cinderella's ball by the end of the week, and we'll consult her then. For now, keep an eye on those things," said Ben.

"And we still don't know where our parents are," reminded Jay. "We saw signs of them in the Catacombs, but they still haven't turned up."

But Mal had a theory about where they could be. "Evie, will you do the honors?" she said, motioning toward the Magic Mirror.

"You think it'll really work this time?" Evie asked.

Mal nodded encouragingly.

Evie held up the Magic Mirror. "Magic Mirror in my hand, show us where the villains stand!"

The mirror swirled, cloudy and gray, and then . . .

There they were: Evil Queen powdering her nose back at her castle, Cruella de Vil pawing through the racks of fur coats for just the right one, and Jafar inspecting a device a goblin had just brought into the shop.

"But how did they get back there?" asked Evie, who sounded as if she didn't quite believe what she was seeing.

"Merlin, right?" Ben guessed, turning to Mal. "They must have been somewhere in the Catacombs nearby when he cast the spell."

"Yeah, I think they were following us out of the tunnels," said Jay. "And they must have overheard us talking. They knew we'd found the talismans."

Mal nodded. "Then Merlin sent everyone back where they belonged, and it must have returned them to the Isle of the Lost."

"If they'd been down there for so long, I wonder why they never found the talismans?" asked Evie.

"Maybe because they didn't have a map?" said Carlos. "Yen Sid said you could be lost down there forever. It *is* called the *Endless* Catacombs."

"Hold on, what's that Jafar's got in his hand?" asked Mal, leaning in for a closer look.

"It's the remote that turns off the dome and lets down the bridge," said Carlos with a groan. "That goblin must have found it in the ditch!"

"Wait—it's broken, though, look, it's cracked in half," said Jay.

"But once it's fixed . . ." said Evie nervously.

Once it was fixed, there was no need to explain what would happen next, thought Mal. The villains would be able to leave the island, and now that they knew who had their talismans, nothing would stop them from heading back to Auradon to take what was theirs.

More than ever, she, Evie, Jay, and Carlos would have to destroy the talismans while Ben prepared the kingdom for a showdown with their enemies on the Isle of the Lost. Ben looked confident, but Mal and her friends weren't as hopeful. They knew how twisted their parents could be, and what they were capable of, and no one would sleep well that night.

"I'm not worried," said Ben. "In Auradon, we can count on our heroes to protect us."

"I don't feel like a hero," said Carlos.

"That's okay," said Mal with a rueful smile. "Remember what the professor said? We're the villains you root for in the story."

acknowledgments

Thank you to the heroic teams at Disney Hyperion, Disney Channel, and Disney Consumer Products, who continue to believe that villains rule! Thanks especially to my ever-patient editors, Emily Meehan and Julie Moody, my awesome publicist, Seale Ballenger, as well as the rest of the fun-loving D-H crew who I'm proud to call my friends: Hannah Allaman, Mary Ann Zissimos, Elena Blanco, Kim Knueppel, Sarah Sullivan, Jackie De Leo, Frank Bumbalo, Dina Sherman, Elke Villa, Andrew Sansone, Holly Nagel, Marybeth Tregarthen, Sara Liebling, Martin Karlow, Dan Kaufman, Marci Senders, James Madsen, and Russ Gray. Thank you to DCP grand pooh-bahs Leslie Ferraro, Andrew Sugerman, Raj Murari, and my dear Jeanne Mosure. Thank you to Channel stars Jennifer Rogers-Doyle, Adam Bonnett, Naketha Mattocks, Laura Burns, Kate Reagan, and Carin Davis.

Thank you to the beautiful young people who star in *Descendants*—Dove Cameron, Sofia Carson, Cameron Boyce, Booboo Stewart, Mitchell Hope, Sarah Jefferey, Brenna D'Amico, Diane Doan, Jedidiah Goodacre, and Zachary Gibson—for being so inspirational, helping promote the book, and for being so nice to my kid at the premiere! Thank you, Kenny Ortega, for making such a fun movie!

Thank you to Richard Abate, Rachel Kim, and everyone at 3Arts. Thank you, Colleen Wilson, for your patient dependability.

Thank you to my awesome DLC-Green-Ong-Gaisano-Torre-Ng-Lim-Johnston family. Thank you to Team A.U.: Margie Stohl and Raphael Simon for the late-night pep talks (texts?). Big love and thanks to Team Yallwest and Yallfest: Tahereh Mafi, Ransom Riggs, Marie Lu, Kami Garcia, Brendan Reichs, Sandy London, Veronica Roth, Leigh Bardugo, Holly Goldberg Sloan, Aaron Hartzler, Ally Condie, Richelle Mead, Patrick Dolan, Andria Amaral, Emily Williams, Steph Barna, Shane Pangburn, Tori Hill, and Jonathan Sanchez, for the laughs and camaraderie. Thank you to my dear family of friends, especially the CH Mama Crew: Jill Lorie, Heidi McKenna, Celeste Vos, Jenni Gerber, Lindsay Nesmith, Maria Cina, Dawn Limerick, Carol Evans, Bronwyn Savasta, Gloria Jolley, Fatima Goncalves, Ava McKay, Nicole Jones, Heather Kiriakou, Kathleen Von Der Ahe, Maggie Silverberg, Dana Boyd, Dana Rees, Heidi Madzar, Angelee Reiner, Vicki Haller,

Betty Balian, Jen Kuklin, Lisa Orlando, Bridget Johnsen, and Tiffany Moon. I love you and your kids and I thank you for all the support during the writing of this book and the one before it (and the one after this!).

Thank you to all the rotten little Descenders! You guys are amazing!

Thanks most to my husband, Mike Johnston, who makes every book of mine so much better and makes me feel like a queen, and to our little princess, Mattie. Thank you to my office buddy, our Maltese, Mimi, who's kept me company through every draft!

Coming in
Summer 2016
A new
Descendants
book series!
SCHOOL
OF
SECRETS